Champagne Lies

Wendy VanHatten

DocUmeant *Publishing*
244 5th Avenue
Suite G-200
NY, NY 10001
646-233-4366
www.DocUmeantPublishing.com

DocUmeant Publishing
244 5th Avenue, Suite G-200
NY, NY 10001
Phone: 646-233-4366

Copy Editor
Corie Barloggi

Cover Design and Layout
Ginger Marks

DocUmeantDesigns.com

Printed in The United States of America
ISBN13: 978-1-937801-40-3
ISBN10: 1-937801-40-3

DEDICATION

To Rick . . . for encouragement and, of course, for Champagne.

ACKNOWLEDGMENTS

Many thanks to Corie for her editing, suggestions, and patience; to all those who read the manuscript and gave me feedback; to my dad for giving me the traveling and writing bug; and for all of you who read this.

PROLOGUE

What the hell? I know I'm not the most graceful person in the world, but I usually don't trip over grains of sand on a well manicured beach. Unless, of course, that sand is piled two feet high smack dab in the middle of that beach. Right where everyone, including me, walks.

Excuse me . . . but what is this doing here?

Can't I enjoy just being out here, watching the sky change colors as the sun sets, and listening to the waves? Why would I look down at my feet? Plus, I walk here all the time at twilight and there's never been anything but an immaculately groomed, sandy beach.

Bending over and looking closer, I discover it really is a heap of who knows what. It's not very neat either. There's sand scattered all over the top of it. Actually, the sand appears to be spread on top of the pile, deliberately trying to cover it. Plus, it's almost in the shadows cast from the sun as it dips behind the condos and resort buildings. No wonder I didn't see it and tripped.

But, who in the world would leave that size of a pile of stuff out here on such a nice expanse of beach? Did someone forget their things? Is it garbage? No, I think it's larger than a bag of garbage. There's no bag that I can see. And, it doesn't smell at all that I can tell. Maybe someone forgot their towels. No, it's much bigger than that. Whatever it is, it shouldn't be here. I just don't get it.

This whole complex with its upscale resort and permanent condos are as good as you'll find along the Mexican Rivera.

I'm talking five stars. Their white sand beaches are pristine . . . even at night. I've seen the beach crew raking, cleaning, and smoothing out every little wrinkle of sand. This pile won't make them happy. And, if it is garbage . . . they'll be really mad, more like pissed off.

Looking around, I see some couples walking hand in hand along the water in the distance. Maybe I should move it away from right here in the middle of the beach so no one else trips. Then, the beach crew can deal with it in the morning. It really is right in the path where everyone walks. And, the sky is getting darker. Pretty soon it will be impossible to see this heap.

I'll just shove it out of the way. Umph . . . that doesn't work. Wait . . . there appears to be a piece of material or something sticking out of the sand. Maybe I can grab that and drag the whole pile out of the way. Bending my legs, I grab it and tug. Huh . . . that doesn't work either. I work out but I'm not into heavy duty lifting so I know I won't be able to pick this up.

With the roar of the surf, it probably wouldn't do any good to call for help, either. No one would hear me anyway. I'll have to try something else.

One more time I dig my bare feet into the sand and tug harder on the material.

But, as I try to move it even a couple of inches, I discover it's more than heavy. It's quite unmanageable. Looking closer, I don't think sand is just on top of it; I think it's partly buried in the sand. That could be why it doesn't budge. I wonder if the material belongs to someone's shirt. Probably some tourist who had too much to drink, stumbled out here, and fell into a heap. That still won't set well with the beach crew.

Clearing some of the sand away from one edge, I grab what appears to be an arm. Maybe this will make whoever it is wake up. Wait . . . it's stiff. Stiff and kind of cold. I wonder how long they've been out here. Days have been hot; well into the 90s. But, nights can get quite cool. This person, if it is a person, must really be out of it.

I tug some more and then all of a sudden it hits me. This motionless pile isn't going anywhere. Dropping what I assume is an arm; I quickly step back and kneel down onto the beach to stare at it. It's not moving at all. What's wrong here? The more I look at it, the more I'm positive it's a person. But, it's definitely not moving. Looking closer, I'm not even sure it's breathing. Could I have just stumbled over a dead body? Yikes . . . a DEAD body?

Somebody help me. Looking in all directions for help, I want to scream but nothing seems to come out of my mouth. What is going on? Why would a dead body be right here? Grabbing my cell phone from my pocket, I call the front office. They can call the police or whoever. . . .

I was having such an enjoyable night, too . . . before all of this.

All previous, pleasant images from my walk on the beach that were in my brain have vanished . . . the sand so soft and cool it could be sugar; the light as it now drifts down from a full moon, enough to illuminate most of the beach and a few wandering couples; the misty spray from gently crashing waves that moisten my face; the ever-present warm wind . . . more like a strong breeze at night.

As I stare at the pile, waiting to talk to the office, I'm numb. Nothing else registers in my brain.

Did I really just trip over a dead body?

1

appy. Happy and excited to be planning our 30th wedding anniversary celebration trip, Jon and I sat on the living room sofa surrounded by brochures and travel books. Dozens of different sites were bookmarked on our tablets . . . his iPad and my Android. Guide books lay strewn all over the floor and coffee table. Remnants of our late lunch were cleared to the side to make room for more maps from all over the world.

Where do we go? How long should we stay? How do we decide? In 30 years we've traveled to so many places. After all, as a travel writer for major magazines, traveling was my work. But, this time . . . it's all for pleasure.

Should we go back to one of our favorite spots or choose a new one?

Remember that B & B in Burgundy? I'd go back there, wander through the vineyards, and sample wines in the caves. Or, how about the apartment in Venice? Venice is one of my favorite cities. Sitting and sipping Venetian Spritzes on the terrace, watching traffic on the Grand Canal, and enjoying the gondolas at sunset. Then again, Provence in the spring has always intrigued me. I love the French Champagne region in fall; I've wanted to visit Brussels but this time in winter; I'd like to see more of the Alps of Austria; the French Riviera is always so relaxing. Spain and Portugal would even be fun to explore some more . . . paella and dancing. Maybe we should do an around the world trip, stopping at several different locations.

And, then I always loved Paris, and Florence, and Tuscany, and Fiji, and New Zealand, and that little place along the Mosel in Germany and . . . Oh my, so many choices. Part of me wants to head back to Oslo and explore where my grandparents came from. But, not in the winter. Much too cold! I may look Scandinavian with my blond hair and blue eyes, but at five foot three inches tall and small build, I don't handle that type of cold very well.

Deciding we need champagne to help us make up our minds, Jon tells me he will walk to the corner liquor store and be back within 10 minutes. Good idea. Champagne makes everything better and so much more fun. As he heads out the door, I glance at the clock. Going to our china cabinet, I reach for our special champagne glasses we bought in Murano, Italy, and place them on the coffee table. Filling the champagne bucket with ice, I set it next to the glasses. Since we both love fresh strawberries with our champagne, I arrange a plate of them and place it next to the glasses. All set now. Looking back at the clock, I figure Jon will be here any minute. I might as well look at a few more brochures and relax while I wait.

And, I wait. And wait. After 45 minutes I'm mildly concerned. Thinking I should call him, I notice his phone is still sitting on the table by the door. In fact, it's sitting right next to his wallet. Guess he'll have to call me from the store for a credit card. That's probably what's taking him so long. Or, he ran into someone he knew and got to talking. We've lived in San Francisco for 30 years . . . in the same house, on the same hill. We know all of our neighbors. Most of them have been here just as long as we have.

Figuring I'll give him another few minutes, I go back to looking at enticing photos of places I want to visit. I could spend hours just looking at them.

First, we should decide the country . . . or at least an area. I'll start a list and narrow that down while I'm waiting for Jon. Next, we should think about the time of year we want to go. When we have traveled for pleasure in the past, we usually went in the spring. But, fall might be a nice change of pace this trip. I'll check airfares for both seasons. That might make a difference, too.

The chiming doorbell causes me look up at the clock again. Two hours? I can't believe it. I had no idea Jon had been gone that long. He must have forgotten his keys, too, or maybe he wants to surprise me by bringing me flowers. Opening the door with a huge grin on my face, I stop short at the sight of two policemen. They do not have huge grins on their faces. My grin disappears.

2

Sitting in a private waiting area in the hospital, I alternately stare at my shaking hands and the gray carpeted floor. I am stunned, shocked, and confused . . . all at the same time. All I've been told by the two policemen at my door and the first doctor I saw is that Jon suffered a massive heart attack and was dead. A heart attack? His annual physical was last week . . . he was in perfect health . . . he was strong as a bull . . . nothing was wrong. Jon, all six foot three inches of him, exercised regularly, ate all the right foods, and looked like the perfect picture of health.

I don't believe them.

Looking around this stark, sparsely furnished, small room at the hospital I try to remember how I got here. I think I followed the police car in my own car. I remember answering the door. I remember grabbing my travel bag, the one I use as a purse when I travel, as it was sitting in the living room next to our travel books. I also remember thinking that the policemen can't possibly be talking about Jon. Who identified him? His wallet was still at home. I'm positive they have the wrong person.

The policemen first told me he was found on the sidewalk over 10 blocks from our house . . . not on the way to or from the corner liquor store where he was supposed to be going. He had no champagne with him.

Now, two different doctors have come in, patted my arm, asked me some questions, and then left. I'm beginning to feel awkward. And, left in the dark. While the doctors are pleasant enough to me, the one remaining policeman acts strange around me. He looks unhappy, actually more like nervous, when I try to ask questions of the doctors. I want to know what Jon was doing so far away from the corner liquor store. Are they positive it was a heart attack? Why can't I see him? Who found him?

I still can't believe it. Is Jon really dead? Am I sure? Is anybody sure? Where is everybody?

I need to see Jon.

In fact, when I take my phone out of my purse, I notice it's been almost an hour. What's going on? Maybe I should try to find someone. The last time I saw Jon, he waved and blew me a kiss as he went out the door. I expected to see him come back through that same door . . . with champagne.

I need some sort of confirmation. Gathering up my travel purse, I head toward the door.

As if on cue, that door opens and an older, different doctor makes an appearance with the same on-edge policeman who was standing outside the door to this small waiting room. Avoiding eye contact and looking over my head, the policeman tells me he is sorry for my loss. He has Jon's belongings . . . what little he had on him . . . in a small, clear plastic bag. Handing it to me, all I see is his gold wedding band, some loose change, a dark gray key ring with a small, round gadget on it, one credit card, and a creased piece of paper with what appears to be a phone number. Not much, as far as belongings go.

Inspecting the plastic bag, several things immediately strike me as odd. One . . . the empty key ring. It wasn't even the key ring I gave him for our anniversary several years ago. I could have sworn he kept all his keys on the same key ring. In fact, I know he did. Why wouldn't he have that key ring? Where did he get this one that's in the plastic bag? I've never seen it before.

Plus, I don't recognize the phone number on the tiny scrap of paper. And, I've never seen that credit card. It has Jon's name and a bank logo on it I don't recognize. Thanking the policeman, I stick the small bag with its contents in my purse.

Asking if they are sure it is Jon, the policeman tells me they used the name on his credit card to figure out who he was. How does that work? No answers. The doctor, much more pleasant than the policeman, asks if I am okay.

Steadying myself, I ask to see Jon. The doctor kindly informs me he will take me to the body. The policeman says he will accompany us. When the doctor tells him it isn't necessary, the policeman says he needs me to make a positive identification. Reluctantly agreeing, the doctor leads me to the elevator that will take us from this area of the hospital down to the morgue. The policeman follows but, again, without making eye contact. Am I ready for this? Maybe it's all a dream and I will wake up once I get off the elevator. Yeah . . . right.

Stepping off the elevator, we walk down a short hallway and through a series of doors. Along the way, a mixture of smells assaults my senses. I concentrate on those . . . rubbing alcohol, antiseptic, bleach, and something else I can't quite seem to identify. I figure if I think about the smells, I won't have to think about why I'm here. That's not really working, however.

Entering a small, cold room with sterile, gray walls, my eyes take in everything. One whole wall consists of numbered drawers, what appear to be work tables or benches line another wall, the ceiling is filled with lights, and gleaming silver tables line up in the center of the room. All the tables are empty except for one. Taking a deep breath, I grab the doorway to steady myself. I have to do this. I can't pass out now . . . maybe I will discover it's not really Jon and everyone has made a huge mistake.

Taking my arm, the doctor leads me to the stainless steel table in the center of the room where a simple white sheet covers what I figure must be a body. The policeman hovers between the doctor and me, looking at me like I've just sprouted another nose. Stepping in front of the doctor and uncovering just the head and shoulders, the policeman asks me to identify the body. I take another deep breath and look. It's Jon . . . looking like he just laid down for a nap.

Sobs come from somewhere all around and then I realize . . . it's me. Reaching out to touch him, the policeman holds my hand back, instructs me to touch only his face, and tells me to not uncover him anymore than he already is. If that seems strange, it doesn't register. With tears running down my cheek, I caress his cool face and gently kiss him . . . goodbye. These few minutes are all I have to bid farewell to Jon, my best friend and husband for over 30 years.

The doctor leads me out of the morgue with the ever-present policeman bringing up the rear. I'm so numb I can hardly stand.

What do we, I mean, what do I do next? How am I supposed to live without Jon? Where do I begin?

3

itting in the front row of the church, I'm beginning to emerge slightly from my rattled world. I had never really been involved in arranging a funeral service before. My parents made their own arrangements years before their accident and I just followed their wishes. It wasn't even like planning an actual funeral.

And, I didn't do much for Jon's, either. It just sort of happened. In fact, I'm not quite sure how this service was put together so quickly. I had very little to do with it. Who set the date? Who brought the food that is now at my house? Did I give someone answers to those questions?

More importantly, who released Jon from the morgue? I thought I had to sign something. I'm sure I didn't. Maybe his attorney did. Then, why did Jon want a closed casket? We never discussed this. I know people think that's odd. Hell, even I think it's odd. I guess I wanted more closure than those few minutes I had been given in the hospital morgue with the ever watchful, crabby looking policeman.

Funeral . . . the word hasn't sunk in yet. One week ago, Jon and I were planning a trip. A celebration. Fun things . . . not funerals. I'm having difficulty making the mental adjustment. Also, the more I sit here listening to our minister talk about Jon and his life, the more questions I have.

I think I'm done crying. I mean how could I have any more tears left? But, I don't know. The only thing I'm sure of is, I'm still numb. I couldn't even tell you what has happened since the police showed up on my doorstep that dreadful afternoon.

My mind wanders some more . . .

What about Jon's parents? Come to think of it . . . I have no idea about Jon's parents. Married for 30 years and Jon never once answered any of my questions about his parents. As I think back, he always had a diversion. Now, I find myself wondering about that. They didn't come to our wedding but sent us money . . . a lot of money. It was enough to buy our home in San Francisco, I do remember that. They have never communicated with us since then . . . at least not that I know of. Jon always told me not to worry . . . if they want to see us, they will. He said they were very private. Again, that seems a lot stranger now than it has for the past 30 years. The minister is still talking . . .

My mind wanders more and I ask myself all sorts of questions. Do you suppose Jon's parents are still alive? If so, shouldn't I tell them their son is dead? If so, how do I do that?

Dead.

I fight back one more sob. Apparently, I'm not finished crying.

The service is finally over. The minister told me Jon wanted a private burial so he has arranged for that. He will let me know when that is. Again, it might have seemed strange if I had thought about it. But, I wasn't really thinking clearly yet.

Finally, back at our home, people walk softly around the living room. Everyone is so pleasant to me yet it seems as if no one wants to disturb me. Friends, co-workers, neighbors, and people I don't think I know or remember all mingle with one another. Their voices are even softer as they drink small glasses of wine, eat small appetizers, and make small talk with each other in between bites. Snippets of whispered conversation sometimes penetrate my numb brain.

"Jon seemed so healthy. I wonder why she wanted a closed casket. How old was he? What's she going to do now? They didn't have any kids, did they? We just played tennis last week and now he is gone. Are they sure it was a heart attack? We need to give her some time and then maybe ask her to dinner. He seemed like he was in great shape. Doesn't it seem odd that he has been gone for only a week and the service was today? When is he going to be buried?"

So many people are here in my house. I smile and nod, having no idea what anyone just said to me. I can't wait until they are all gone and I can sit and reflect by myself. I really don't want pity or sympathy. Right now, I just want to be left alone. Alone with my memories of Jon, my thoughts, and my many questions. Before too long, I'm saying goodbye to everyone, thanking them for coming, and reassuring them I will be fine.

As I walk around my, now empty, house I notice someone cleaned up and left everything spotless. I think I thanked them . . . but I'm not sure. Several people asked me what I was going to do. I don't know. What am I going to do? I have so many questions and the more I try to answer them . . . the more questions I have. So much confusion.

Another small sob bubbles to my lips as I wander through the living room and end up sitting on the sofa where Jon and I were planning our trip. Was that really only a week ago?

Now that everyone is gone, I just want to sit by myself for a bit. So, I sit. I think. I still can't make sense of anything; why Jon died, what to do next, and my conversation with Jon's attorney yesterday. After what seems like an hour, I realize that thinking and rethinking is going nowhere and giving me nothing but a headache. Never being one to dwell on things I can't solve, I decide to treat all of it like the puzzle it is. Jon loved puzzles and taught me to love them too.

What I need is my journal to help me record my questions, decide my plans, and begin to move forward. I work better when I can write down all my thoughts and questions. Since they are in my office at the back of the house and since it's beginning to get dark, I'll close the drapes as I head back there. Then, with a journal and a pen, I can start on my list. That gives me a purpose.

As I begin to close the drapes in the living room, I glance outside and notice a dark colored car sitting by the curb. I probably wouldn't have even seen it had I not noticed the headlights in the twilight. *Hmm . . . I thought everyone was gone.* When I pause long enough to look more closely, they speed off. *Wonder what that was all about. Typically, this is a very quiet neighborhood. Did they see me looking at them? Whatever . . .*

Continuing on to my office, I allow myself one more good cry as I walk through the house. Back in the living room, with my journal in hand, I take a deep sigh to clear out the fuzziness in my brain. Sitting down on the sofa, I begin to get comfortable.

First journal entry . . . the call I received about Jon's will.

4

Robert A. Jonse, who identified himself as Jon's attorney, called yesterday to tell me he had Jon's will. He said he would come to the house and fill me in on the details. That way I wouldn't have to come downtown.

I knew Jon had a will. In fact, we both had wills. But, Mr. Jonse wasn't our regular attorney. Still, he had documents from Jon. I invited him to the house and immediately liked him when I met him.

But, when he explained the will to me yesterday afternoon, I was confused. Telling him this wasn't the will I thought Jon had and that this one was entirely different than the one I remembered we had with a Mr. Fleetwood. This one seemed longer, more specific, and much more detailed. Of course, everything was in perfect order. It shouldn't have surprised me since Jon was an engineer and a very orderly person. Still, I didn't understand. Several things surprised me, confused me, and shocked the hell out of me. Again, more questions than answers.

First, I had never met Mr. Jonse. How did he even know Jon was dead? I forgot to ask him that. But, he must have known Jon for quite some time because he certainly knew a lot about Jon and his life. He seemed to know all about me, too, but funny thing, I had never heard

Jon mention Mr. Jonse's name. Thirty years and I didn't know Jon had an attorney other than Mr. Fleetwood, who I thought was our family attorney. I didn't know Jon even had a second will. Strange.

Mr. Jonse also told me Jon's assistant, Shelly, called to let him know Jon's office had already been cleaned out and a moving company would be bringing a dozen or so boxes to the house. Boxes . . . boxes of what? I had been in Jon's office. If I remember correctly, all of Jon's office things could fit in one or two small boxes. I think hiring a moving company is a little overkill.

Plus, how did that happen so quickly? Apparently, Jon's boss is out of town for a month and couldn't talk to me. I guess I will have to wait to talk to him. In the meantime I need to talk to Shelly to see what else I need to do about Jon's office or any of Jon's documents.

Finally, Mr. Jonse showed me the amount of money Jon left for me. I'm sure my mouth actually hung open. Where on earth did Jon accumulate all that money? He had a good job and I kept our finances in order. We didn't exactly worry about money. But, we certainly were not wealthy. Until, that is, Mr. Jonse explained the trust fund Jon set up for me in case of his death.

Wealthy doesn't begin to describe the amount of money in that account. I'm not sure that many zeroes will ever register in my mind. Plus, access is not restricted. It's all mine. Available now, according to Mr. Jonse, the attorney I didn't know existed before this week. There is so much money; I can't begin to fathom it right now.

Mr. Jonse also suggested I not mention I inherited this large of an amount of money to anyone. No kidding? Who would believe me, anyway? Before he left my house, he told me he would be getting all the documents in order for me to sign. They would probably all be completed in about a month. He told me I could call his assistant to set up an appointment at his office downtown. Nodding, I agreed.

Maybe I need to start another section in my journal to make sense of all this. My head is spinning just thinking about his visit and the will. I swear I only had one glass of wine after everyone left the house following the funeral service.

The more I think, the more things just don't seem to add up. What am I missing . . . besides Jon?

Telling myself it's time to stop dwelling on things I don't know and go on to make lists of things I really do know, I start yet another page.

But, first where are Jon's car keys?

5

Wow. Where has the last month gone? It seems like only yesterday we were both sitting right here on the sofa making our travel plans. Looking over my journals, I discover I've actually accomplished quite a few things. I've started cleaning and slowly getting rid of Jon's things, I've made some adjustments in my routine, and I'm functioning better at being alone.

After all, who knew there were so many details to take care of when someone dies? Plus, the shock of Jon dying so suddenly has begun to wear off. I know Jon is gone. No longer is he coming in the front door with his jaunty, "Honey, I'm home", greeting; and, I'm trying to adjust to life without Jon.

Sitting on the floor in our walk-in closet, I'm cleaning out more of Jon's things and placing them in boxes for donation. Finished with his tennis clothes and gear, casual clothes, shoes, shorts, t-shirts, and other odds and ends, this whole process is getting easier the more I deal with it. I have several boxes of things ready to go to the Veterans' Donation Center. Jon and I always supported anything to do with veterans and animals. I'm sure the Vets' Center can sell these things in their thrift store. It's all in excellent condition.

But, I can't quite bring myself to go through all of his suits and give them away yet. One week at a time. Then I will rearrange the closet spaces.

I was hoping to find his car keys and the key ring I had given him. Since I have my set of keys, I could at least use his car if I needed to. It's not one I regularly drive, though. I guess I'll look for the keys later.

Okay, enough cleaning for now. Walking from our bedroom to my office, I suddenly have an eerie sensation that someone is watching me. I can't quite pinpoint it, but I feel like I should look over my shoulder. In fact, I can feel the hair on the back of my neck stand up. But, when I finally do look, no one is there. Good. . . .

It's slowly turning to dusk so my lights in the house are on but I haven't closed all of the drapes yet. Still, our house has enough shrubbery that people passing by outside can't just look inside and see me. It's probably just my imagination in overdrive. . . .

Ignoring that feeling, I think back to last night's call from my best friend, Marissa. She has been asking me over and over again to take some time and come relax in her condo in Mexico. Until now, I didn't know if I could handle traveling alone again. Maybe it's time I did. I could always reflect, try to come to the finality of Jon's death, and celebrate our life together.

I have a feeling I don't know everything about Jon's heart attack. Maybe I never will. And, maybe that's okay. We had 30 wonderful years together. I need to concentrate on those. As I think about our years together, I remember things I wish I had asked Jon and things I now wish I knew about his life before we met. Come to think of it, there were some gaps about his life he never filled in for me.

What did we talk about? It seemed like we had no secrets from each other, until I really think back. What subjects did he avoid whenever I brought them up? His parents. Okay . . . there were things I wanted to know about his parents, his college years, and his work trips that didn't include me. Were there more parts of his life that he didn't share? Were we really married for 30 years? How could I not know this about my own husband? I'm observant. As a well respected travel writer, I have to be. Things don't just escape me.

Still . . .

A trip to a nice resort area might just help me sort through everything and finally put my questions to rest. At some point, I have to move on. Maybe it's time for me to do that. . . .

I'll call Marissa and let her know I'm coming for the month. She will be in Africa on a photo safari for some magazine and will be glad someone is staying in her condo. If I know Marissa, it's an upscale condo with all the amenities. Probably has things I didn't even know I wanted! And, she will stock it with the finest wines, foods, and gadgets for me to use.

As I sit at the computer in my office making plane reservations for my trip, I realize I need my passport. Even though Jon and I used our passports regularly, he wanted them kept in a small fire proof box in the closet. I hadn't really thought about that when I was cleaning Jon's things out of there. In fact, the last time I thought about passports, Jon was sitting next to me on the sofa. With a long sigh, I realize we didn't get as far as actually booking our plane reservations.

Back to the closet I go. Squatting down and opening the hidden door in the back corner, I reach for the small, dark gray, steel box. It seems to be wedged in tightly but with a good yank, it plops out onto the closet floor. Goodness, it seems heavy. Heavier than I remember. But, Jon was always the one to get it out and open it. I certainly don't think I could carry it very far. And, it's no bigger than the shoe box my boots fit in.

Grabbing the key from my jewelry box, I drag the box out into the light of our bedroom to unlock it. All I need is my passport. Then I can try to shove it back into its place in the corner of the closet. Since it's as good a place as any, I'll probably still keep it there. As I think about it, *I thought the only things we kept in here were our passports, copies of our wills, and the deed to our house. This must be one sturdy box. That's probably why Jon bought it.*

6

Unlocking the box, our familiar blue passports lay right on top. I'm not sure what to do with Jon's passport, though. It's not as if he will ever need it again. Plus, I can't believe I will ever need it for anything either. Still, I hate to just throw it away. Maybe I should call the passport office here in San Francisco and ask what I am supposed to do with it.

Thinking I'll keep it until I have a chance to call them, I decide to look at the deed to the house. It's here in its familiar brown envelope. Next to it are two official looking white envelopes containing our wills. Hmm . . . I sort of forgot about this will of Jon's. It's odd that our attorney, the one we had together, Mr. Fleetwood, hasn't called me.

Do I open it? If I remember correctly, these are only copies. Mr. Fleetwood has the originals. Or, at least I think he has them in his office. Do I wait for instructions from him? Or, should I call Mr. Fleetwood's office to see what I need to do with Jon's? Then again, I wonder if he knows about Jon's other will and other attorney, Mr. Jonse. Glancing at the clock on my nightstand I decide it's too late to call now. I guess I will have to call Mr. Fleetwood in the morning to see if there is anything new I should know about this will. I think

I know what it says . . . but after the last one, I can't be too sure of anything.

That appears to be the entire contents in our box. My expensive jewelry is locked away in a special compartment of my dresser. Jon was insistent I keep all of it where I could access it easily and wear it when we went out. He said there was no need to put any of my jewelry in this box where he would have to bring it out every time I wanted to wear any of it. Because he loved buying me nice rings and necklaces, I have quite a bit of it.

One thing though . . . I never realized this box was so heavy. I wonder why? I had trouble just sliding it around on the carpet to get it out into the light of the bedroom. Looking at it, it sure seems a lot bigger on the outside than the small space inside where our documents are sitting. I mean, fireproof is good. But, this seems a little ridiculous. Guess I never noticed that before. Or, since Jon was always the one to get our passports out before we went on a trip, I guess I never paid much attention to it. Perhaps I should take a closer look at this heavy box.

Taking out the three envelopes and both of our passports, I notice a tiny red button on the floor of the box. Maybe there's a secret compartment! Or, maybe it has a false bottom. Ha . . . that would be just like Jon to hide my next Christmas present where I couldn't find it. He knew I liked to search the house for his hiding spots.

Perhaps I'll find the last gift of jewelry he ever bought for me. Wouldn't that be special? I would cherish it forever.

Well, no time like the present to find what I'm sure is my special gift of jewelry. Pushing on the button, nothing happens. Hmm. I try again, pressing down a little harder, I hear a distinctive click and the top slowly opens.

Oh . . . My . . . God. . . .

It's a good thing I'm sitting on the floor or I might have fallen over. In fact, I still might. . . .

Shutting the lid carefully, disbelieving what I just saw, I close my eyes for an instant thinking maybe it will all disappear. Nope. The box is still here, right in front of me. Okay. Maybe if I reopen it, everything inside will have changed.

Slowly, I lift the lid for a second time and the surprising contents are still staring back at me. Definitely, not the gift of expensive jewelry I was hoping to find.

7

Four more passports lay scattered on top of the pile; all blue ones. What? Why so many? That's not all. Money . . . several neat stacks of money, bound together with rubber bands, rest next to the passports. I wonder how much is here.

Then, looking closer I see the reason this small box is so heavy. Gold . . . well, I assume it's gold . . . haphazardly covers the bottom of the box. My mouth hangs open in disbelief. What the hell?

What is gold doing in our box? Is this legal? Where did this come from? Who else knows it is here? What were you doing with this, Jon? What do I do with this?

Confusion, then anger, and back to confusion . . . I don't know what to do. Jon . . . what is this? What have you done? Why aren't you here so I can ask you about this? I'm dizzy.

A small sob escapes my lips as I realize I have so many more new questions. More puzzles pieces when I thought I was finding answers. Okay. I tell myself to take a deep breath and focus. It seems like that's all I've been doing since Jon died.

I probably need to document everything that's in here. I don't know why, but it seems like the thing to do. I'm sure no one will believe me . . . it's all surreal. Getting up off the bedroom floor, I'm shaky as

I walk to my office to grab my camera. I could be dreaming . . . right?

Once back in my bedroom, I take photos of the box and its contents as it sits on the floor. Then, I spread out all the passports and take photos of those. Inspecting them closer, I pick up the first one and notice Jon's photo inside. It's him, alright. But, wait a minute. It has a different name, address, birth date, and place of birth. What's up with that? Looking at the next two, I see Jon's photo in these as well. Again, each has a different name, address, and birth date. Why wouldn't they all be the same? Why would he need these? Where did he get them? I thought you could only have one passport. Isn't there some kind of law like that?

Flipping through them, I see they all have passport stamps. It appears he actually used these . . . Rome, Madrid, Hanoi, Amsterdam, Frankfurt, Florence, and more. Many more.

Even more confusing is the fact that one of the stamps is from as recently as eight months ago. Eight months ago! I didn't know he was in Hanoi eight months ago. I didn't even know he had ever been to Hanoi. Where was I? What was he doing in Hanoi? Why didn't he tell me about it? What was I doing that I wouldn't have noticed him being gone? His company doesn't have business in Hanoi that I'm aware of. What the hell is going on?

Then I notice the last passport. Probably more of the same, I think, as I pick it up. But, big surprise as I open that one.

It has my photo in it, but not my name. It has a different name, different date of birth than my actual one, and different place of birth. Huh? I never applied for this one. What is it doing here? Is it really me? It sure looks like me. . . . Now, I'm beyond confused. I'm scared and paranoid, all at the same time. Jon . . . what have you done? Who are you? If you were here, I'd tell you exactly how pissed off I am at you right now.

I snap some more photos of the insides of all the passports and then move on to the money. I grab a nearby towel from the bathroom and carefully lay all of it out on that. I have no idea how much is here, but I do see there are $100 bills on top of each stack. There are 10 stacks in all, each about four inches high. It could be a lot of money if they are all hundreds. I'll count it later.

Again, more questions. Why would Jon hide this? For that matter, where did he get this money and why did he have it? Thinking maybe it was perhaps a 'rainy day fund', why didn't he tell me about it? But, why wouldn't he have it in our bank account? We have several savings accounts, all for different things.

Focus . . .

Snapping some more photos of the stacks of money, I think I'll ask Mr. Fleetwood what he knows about this. I mean, who else would I ask? It seems an attorney should know these things. Right?

Now I want to look at the gold bars . . . if it really is gold. Come to think of it, I've never actually seen gold this way. My gold is always in jewelry . . . bought by Jon.

Taking photos of the six small gold bars and dozens of gold coins as they sit scattered on the bottom of the box, I begin to wonder if all this is happening. This can't possibly be real, can it? Am I awake? I certainly feel awake. What is all of this doing in our house? Did Jon know it was here? Of course he did. Apparently, he put it here. But, when? And, why?

What the heck am I going to do with it? I can't just take it to the bank and say "look what I found in the closet", can I? Definitely, I need to wait until morning and call our attorney. I really do hope he has some answers. I'm getting real tired of questions.

Keeping my 'real' passport out, I carefully replace the stacks of money and the extra passports. I feel like I need to put it back the way I found it but I'm not sure why. Who's going to care? Plus, the gold coins slide around as I'm replacing everything. Jostling the coins around so I can close the lid . . . I gasp in more disbelief.

Just how many surprises can I take in one day?

8

Small, yet ominous looking, sits a dark grey hand gun, staring up at me from under the gold coins. I didn't see it before as it's about the same color as the bottom of the box. And I was concentrating on the shiny gold. Now, I'm no longer curious and confused. I'm scared. And, I'm getting more pissed off at Jon by the minute.

Looking around the bedroom I feel like I'm in some sort of poorly written spy movie. Again, I feel like someone is watching me. Did I lock the front door? Telling myself to 'stop it', I hastily put everything back inside and lock the box. This is more than surreal. It's now turned into scary.

Okay. I need to get a grip and stop all this nonsense. No, I think I need a drink!

Seriously, I do need to talk to our attorney about all of this. He can help me with the legal ramifications and tell me what to do with everything here. I certainly don't have a clue what I should do with any of it.

I came in here to retrieve my passport. Now it's time for me to shove this heavy box back in its original hiding spot, replace the key, and finish making my plane reservations for Mexico. I need to get my mind off everything that has happened tonight. I'll deal with all of it later.

Taking my passport to my office, I complete my reservations and head back to my bedroom. It's late and I really need to get some sleep. Hopefully, I can make sense of all of this in the morning after I talk to my attorney.

But, after a restless night's sleep, my call to Mr. Fleetwood is not a productive one. His assistant tells me he is out of the country for a while but I can set up an appointment in a few weeks to a month. She's not sure when he will return. She is not someone I recognize but she might be new since the last time I've actually contacted his office. When she asks what my business is, I tell her it's confidential. I only tell her I need help answering several questions.

She's pushy. Asking me to give her more information, I briefly explain that it has to do with Jon's death as well as his will. She wants more specifics. I sidestep the question and tell her I found a copy of Jon's will and I just want to talk to Mr. Fleetwood about it. She persists, in a demanding tone. Increasingly, I don't like the way her tone is going or the fact that she's even questioning me for that matter. She's too nosey and too harsh for my taste.

Since I won't discuss any of this on the phone with a complete stranger, I politely tell her I will speak only to Mr. Fleetwood about these issues. She appears to be miffed at me. Oh well. It's really none of her business.

Finally, she sets up a tentative appointment six weeks from today. Frustrated with the conversation, I try to put it out of my mind as I hang up.

Now, I really do have to pack. My plane leaves SFO early tomorrow morning. Checking the Mexican weather forecast for the next month, it makes my packing a whole lot easier.

Swimsuits, shorts, tank tops, and a few sundresses don't take up much room. Throw in a few flip flops, sandals, my camera, my laptop, my bathroom necessities, and a shawl . . . and I'm ready to go. I add my journal with my questions and put my suitcase and my travel purse by the door.

Making a call to our neighbor down the street, I tell him I am going to be gone for about a month. I ask him to get my mail and keep an eye on things around my house. Even though this is a very nice neighborhood, we all look out for each other when any of us are away. He's used to us coming and going. Now, he'll get used to just me coming and going. Plus, I do the same for him.

Mexico . . . here I come.

Relaxation . . . it's time. Finally.

9

Ahh, Mexico. Marissa was right. Nothing like sun and sand to restore my sanity. This is exactly what I needed in order to regenerate and to come to terms with Jon's death and everything that has happened since.

But, I just can't believe my month here is about over. It has been glorious. Week one, I just sat, read, and enjoyed the sunshine. I'm not even sure I thought about much except what restaurant to go to and what kind of margarita I should have with my dinner. Talk about relaxing.

Week two I ventured into town and did some shopping. New swimsuits, sandals, and sundresses were added to my wardrobe. Walking on the beach everyday helped me relax and get my mind back into gear. I even found a wine bar located at one of the resorts at the end of this beach. They serve wonderful wines from all over the world, including one of our favorites from California!

During the last two weeks, I've really come to terms with my life and the way it is. Now, sitting out on the palm tree shaded patio overlooking turquoise water, I've come to some more conclusions. This month has been good for me in so many ways. I have had time to relax, while sitting on the brilliant, white sandy beach drinking freshly squeezed limeade, reading a book. Marissa left me a stack of books, telling me to donate them to the reading room when I finished with them. I'm just about completely through the whole pile. Romance novels to tips from marketing gurus . . . I've read a wide variety of genres this past month.

While watching couples walk hand in hand along the edge of the incoming surf, I've also had time to think. That thinking allowed me to develop some plans, including moving on without Jon . . . yet not forgetting about him and our life together.

Some of those plans also include my life as a writer and what I've been doing for the past 30 years. Since I'm still a featured writer for several magazines, I've been receiving emails about upcoming assignments. I've had the chance to look over those and decide what I want to do next.

I've organized what questions I still have, I'll find answers to those that I can, and leave the rest alone. I'm sure Jon would want me to go on with my life. There really is no point in dwelling on things. We had 30 wonderful years and I will always cherish them.

Now, I need to get back to traveling and writing for the magazines. Not only does that give me purpose, but it is what I have always enjoyed. Time to get on with my life . . . my new life.

Plus, I've also come to terms with the fact that Jon provided very well for me. In fact, it's much better than well. I'm wealthy and I can handle that.

I think I'm going to research starting a foundation . . . just not sure what direction yet. I need to get all my ducks in a row before I start giving money away. I have so much more money than I need, so I'd like to find the right place to do some good with it. But, at the same time, I am careful about saying or doing anything with that much money. It's on my list of questions to discuss with Mr. Fleetwood when I see him. Hopefully, he can help me decide where to start.

As I sit in the shade, my drink in hand, my mind wanders. One thing bothered me last night at the restaurant. Perhaps I'm just becoming a little melodramatic and paranoid about one particular man. I could have sworn that he seemed to be watching me all throughout dinner. Whenever I would look his way, he'd glance away from me in a hurry. Almost like he was stalking me. And, I'd bet money that he was the same man I saw a few days ago at the pool. He seemed to be watching me then, too. Both times he gave me the creeps. He probably preys on women tourists that are alone, thinking they're wealthy.

Oh well, my time is about up here. I won't see him anymore. He can find some other woman to watch. I'm not going to let him ruin my last days here.

Walking back inside the condo, I realize I need to start cleaning up all of my things and pack my suitcase. I need to get back to San Francisco. Like Marissa said, I will donate all the books to the local library or reading room here. The housekeeper will take care of any leftover food and wine and get the condo ready for Marissa to return from Africa.

I'll help do what I can before I leave by watering the plants, straightening up everything, stripping the beds, and doing my laundry before I head to the airport in two days. This month has flown by. Afraid that I would be drowning in my own crying fits, I can't believe how much emotional progress I've made. I feel like I am back on the right track towards living. Even if it is minus Jon.

And, my lists are organized with thoughts, questions, and things to do upon my return. I'll call Mr. Fleetwood, first, to get some answers from him. Then, I will finish cleaning out the rest of Jon's clothes and suits and donate them to the veteran's shelter. I'll deal with the rest of Jon's things that I really don't want to keep. Finally, I will deal with the box in our bedroom closet. Once all of that is finished, I can get back some semblance of my life without Jon.

I will enjoy these last couple of days and nights, here on the beach, as much as possible. Sunrises come early but have provided me with amazing photo opportunities. Even though I probably have taken hundreds of photos, a couple more shots wouldn't hurt. I never tire of watching the sun rise and set. And, I think I'll order take out from my favorite restaurant so I can eat among the flowers on the patio. Tomorrow night I'll do the same.

First, tonight calls for a toast to Mexico and helping me heal.

10

My last night. Sitting on the patio, listening to the surf, I'm in a mellow mood as I think about Jon. We had a wonderful life. That sounds like a cliché . . . but it's true. Watching the sky turn from cloudless, almost neon blue to the typical darker shade of royal blue as the sun sets behind me, I reflect on our life together. Raising my glass of dry white wine, I salute Jon. . . .

In some ways, it now seems like a fairy tale.

Jon was an engineer with a successful firm. His house, his car, his life were all well organized. Nothing was out of place and everything had its own place. Priorities and goals were just part of Jon's way of life. And, those included keeping things orderly. He worked hard, yet enjoyed traveling with me when he had the time.

I, on the other hand, was only organized in some areas of my life. Graduating from college, I landed several assignments with a major travel magazine. I was their 'go to travel writer' for many places in Europe, especially Italy. That worked for me. I loved traveling, I loved writing, and I loved the magazine. I could pick up and go at a moment's notice. They paid me well, so it worked for both the magazine and for me. However, organizing my life wasn't high on my priority list. Ask me how to pack for two weeks in Italy and

Croatia . . . and I can tell you. Ask me where my notes are from a trip to Amsterdam . . . and I can tell you. But, ask me where I put yesterday's mail . . . and I have no idea.

Traveling is where I met Jon. It brought us together. I was on assignment in Florence and Jon was taking a couple of extra days in Italy before heading back to the states. He had just been in Rome for work. Hmm . . . I can't seem to remember what his firm was doing in Rome. But then again, that was over 30 years ago.

Jon was standing in front of the Duomo, looking back over his shoulder like he was searching for someone. I bumped into him . . . literally. When I'm trying to take the perfect photo, I sometimes get distracted and don't look where I'm going. Almost knocking him over, I apologized several times . . . in English and then in Italian. He just kept staring at me. And, looking over both shoulders. I figured he spoke neither language and wondered what the heck I was saying.

Finally he looked around, grabbed my arm, and pulled me toward a sidewalk café a couple of shops away. Not sure what was going on, I told him to forget it and started to move away. Smiling at me, he now apologized . . . in English. He said he was distracted and should have moved out of my way, as it was obvious I was busy taking photos. Suggesting we start over, he ordered espressos and apologized again.

We talked for over an hour. How could I ever forget that smile as he asked me all sorts of questions? He was so interested in my work . . . he found it fascinating to meet someone who actually wrote the articles he had read. Now that I think about it, whenever I would ask questions about him, he always directed them back to me.

Finally, I learned his name was Jon and he was an engineer taking a couple of days to see Florence. I offered to show him around, and for the next two days we toured the city together. I was the guide . . . he was the tourist. From museums to churches . . . I showed him just the highlights. Telling him he would have to come back another time to really get to know Florence, he promised he would.

Indulging in mid-morning gelato, eating dinner in back alley trattorias, drinking espresso until midnight, and then sipping limoncello . . . we ate and drank our way around Florence. Two days flew by so fast; it was soon time for him to catch his flight back to the states. He promised to call me . . . and I thought 'yeah, right'.

Two days later my phone rang. Jon was back in the states and wondered when I would be back. Never once had he told me where he lived or worked. When he mentioned he had a condo in San Francisco, I was shocked. That was my home base and where I had my small apartment. Who knew?

We had the typical whirlwind courtship and were married eight months later. Thinking back, even my parents approved of Jon and our short engagement.

With Jon's parents' wedding gift, we bought a beautifully restored home overlooking the San Francisco Bay. In a terrific neighborhood, it was the perfect house. I know it was expensive, but Jon assured me their gift of money completely paid for it. He told me they wanted to do that for us. And, he was right. We never had a mortgage.

Jon wanted a few minor renovations completed before we moved in. Thinking back, I really don't remember what those were. Now, it really doesn't matter. Shortly after our wedding, the work on the house was completed, we moved in, and have been there ever since. It's home.

Jon worked. I continued to write for a couple of magazines. We explored San Francisco together. Life was good; really good. When I had assignments in Europe, Jon would find time to travel with me. We explored the world together.

Thinking about all of that now . . . it does seem like a fairy tale.

We also had our share of bumps, though. Jon would need to go out of town for a week or two and I was never able to accompany him. Not once in 30 years. It was business, he said. That does seem odd now that I think about it. He almost always came with me.

There were times, however, when he would spend only a day with me and wander off to another city for a day or so, alone. Telling me I wouldn't miss him and that he would be back never really bothered me. Until now. Thinking back, those times now seem odd and confusing to me. Did he not want to be with me? Or, was there something else? I don't know . . . probably never will know.

When my parents died in a car accident, Jon comforted me. But, he wanted no investigation into their deaths. Again, that didn't bother me at the time. Why dredge up more hurt? Now . . . I wonder what really happened. The official report was that they were hit head on by a drunk driver on a remote stretch of road along Lake Tahoe. Come to think of it, it was a road they never traveled. Not even once in all the years they lived along the other side of the lake. Mom didn't like that road. She said it was scary. I really don't think Dad would have ever driven it with Mom in the car. I'm not sure what made it scary . . . but Mom definitely didn't like it.

Maybe the wine is causing me to reminisce about all the past incidents in my life!

Speaking of reminiscing, I still haven't told Jon's parents he is dead. But, I have no idea how to contact them. Jon said they knew how to get in touch with us, though. It seems wrong to wait for them to call then say, 'by the way . . . your son is dead', doesn't it? That's a question I initially didn't have for our attorney, but I will put it on my list.

I'm glad that I can at least think about our time together and smile . . . not cry.

My wine is gone. It's promising to be a perfect night with a full moon as soon as the sun sets. I am all packed and ready to go to the airport in the morning. Time to go for one last walk on the beach.

11

A DEAD body…oh my.

Honestly, I can't believe the events of these last couple of hours. What started out as the perfect ending to the perfect month has turned upside down with no warning. My refreshing wine, the colorful sunset, the soothing noise of the never ending waves, the cool sand under my feet . . . it was all perfect. That's the only word for it. Perfect.

Until now. Now it's confusing and scary all at the same time. Why did I have to be the one to find the body? Why did I have to touch it? Yuck.

I hope the police don't think I knew this person. I don't even want to look at him . . . or her.

My questions go unanswered as they swirl around in my mind and I look along the beach for help. Help from whom, I'm not sure. I don't know what to do next. The police told me to wait here for a few more minutes, but I have no idea how long ago that was.

Plus, I can't seem to stop shaking. What is taking the police so long to look at it? Why am I still here?

The more I think, the more upset and irrational I become. Can I just hit rewind and start this evening all over again?

Oh dear . . . I'm making myself crazy the more I question the whole night.

Looking to my right, I see a couple of Mexican policemen headed my way. They have very stern looks on their faces. Am I in trouble?

12

I'm confused. I'm shaking. I'm crying. Hell, I'm surprised I even know my own name right now. I'm not real sure the Mexican Police believe a word I'm saying. At least they speak English. I don't think my Spanish would impress them at this point.

How many times are they going to ask me my name? How many times do I need to tell them what I found? If they would just let me go back to my condo, I could give them the necessary documentation they're asking for. I mean, after all, who walks on the beach at 7 o'lock at night with a purse, a passport, and identification?

Maybe if I could just stop crying hysterically. Better yet, maybe if I could just wake up and have all this be a dream.

A couple of hours later, standing next to the policemen after the body has been bagged and removed, I take a deep breath and try to explain what I'm doing here. Again. Am I on vacation? Sort of. Do I own the condo? No. Where is the owner? In Africa. Where? I'm not sure. Why don't I have any identification? Because it's now 9 o'lock at night. Again, I try to explain to the policemen exactly what I'm doing here . . . but it sounds bizarre even to my ears.

I tell them I am recuperating after my husband's sudden death. When asked what he died of, I let them know it was supposedly a massive heart attack. When questioned about the autopsy, I truthfully answer that there wasn't one. It all sounds kind of lame as I say everything out loud.

Why would the Mexican police ask about an autopsy? That sure seems odd.

I'm so overwhelmed by all of this I can't even stand anymore. So I plop down on the sand, my head in my hands.

One policeman tells me they need to make some calls and for me not to leave Mexico. I tell him my plane leaves in the morning as I need to go back to San Francisco. Nodding and telling me to sit right here, he turns to have a lengthy conversation with his partners.

What on earth is going on? I realize it's not every day a tourist finds a dead body on the beach, especially in this area of expensive condos and resorts. But why do I feel like a criminal? And why are there so many police here? Maybe they don't get much of this kind of action and it's sort of like practice for them. This is an exclusive area. I'm sure they have their share of tourists or condo owners who lose things or need assistance finding their way downtown or get lost. But, probably not a lot of dead bodies.

The nice policeman makes his way back to where I'm sitting and kneels down next to me. He wants my contact information in San Francisco and he wants to make sure I am available to take his phone calls once I get home. He understands I have tickets and doesn't want me to have to forfeit those. He tells me he is glad I reported the body and he hopes I had a relaxing stay while I was here.

As he stands and helps me up, he hands me a business card, and tells me to make sure I have a lawyer back in the U.S. who can deal with what I just found. One who understands Mexican law. He doesn't think I will have to return as long as I have a good lawyer. Just in case . . . he tells me.

Just in case what?

13

⬥━⬥━⬥━⬥━⬥━⬥

Flying first class allows me some space and some time to myself after the unbelievable events of last night. Sitting next to me, a nice gentleman looks up and occasionally smiles; then goes back to working on his laptop. He doesn't bother me and I don't bother him. Good.

I take the opportunity to add some more questions in my journal for Mr. Fleetwood. Specifically . . . what can he do for me in Mexico? And . . . why on earth do I need an attorney there, anyway? All I did was find a dead body. I'm sure the police are just being thorough.

By the time I get settled back home, Mr. Fleetwood will have returned from his vacation and we can set up an appointment. If I remember correctly, his assistant already set a tentative one for me. I'll have to call and confirm that. Best to move ahead with everything as soon as I can. There's a magazine that wants to send me to Venice for a week. Apparently the America's Cup will be doing a preliminary race there. They are looking for a series of articles through the eyes of race followers. Next, they have set up some cooking classes in Sienna they want me to cover. Maybe I'll learn some new Italian dishes at the same time.

All in all, I need to get things in order so I can be gone for a total of three weeks. It feels good to have a purpose again. I know Jon will be with me in spirit. He loved Italy, even though he didn't always stay with me the whole time. I guess he liked exploring on his own and not sticking to my schedule. It was pleasure for him . . . work for me.

Hearing the ding, I look up from writing. Our captain announces we will be starting our initial descent shortly and the flight attendants come by to ask if we want something more to drink or eat. Wow. That seemed like a quick flight. My seat companion orders a sparkling water and introduces himself to me.

Nice looking, friendly in a good way, and about my age, he tells me he's a private investigator who retired from a special branch of the FBI several years ago. When I ask about his FBI career, he mostly glosses over it but tells me his unit tracked unsavory characters. I'm impressed. He says his career was interesting for a long time. But, when it became too much of a job, he decided it was time to leave. Now he works for himself and his clients are high end, high profile people who require his discreet, well informed services.

Apparently, this is more interesting and pays much better. Go figure. As we buckle our seat belts and put our trays away, he hands me his business card. I glance at his name and smile. Telling him thanks, his card goes in my travel purse with my journal. Remaining garbage is collected, we recognize the San Francisco Bay out the window, and we feel the landing gear engage.

Turning and looking me in the eyes, he tells me he has a feeling that I will be visiting with him very soon. He looks serious . . . very serious. Smiling at him, a little uneasy, I just nod. We feel the plane touch down.

Once our plane is at the gate and the flight attendant announces it is okay, we stand to retrieve our carryon luggage from the overhead compartment. Again, he tells me he will see me soon. Not sure what to make of this, I smile and nod once more. Is he coming on to me? He's nice enough but I'm not really interested in that type of relationship right now. I'm not sure if I ever will be again.

Shaking my hand and telling me he was glad to meet me, he leaves the jet way area in one direction as I head the opposite way to baggage claim. Looking at my hand, I realize he left another business card. Okay . . . I get it. He wants me to have his phone number.

Looking at this card, I notice it's not his. It belongs to the attorney Jon had. The one I didn't know about . . . Mr. Robert Jonse.

Chills run down my spine. Coincidence? I honestly don't know. Hmm . . .

14

After a good night's sleep in my own bed, I grab my much needed coffee, unpack, put most of my things away, and start on my 'to do' list. I make a call to Mr. Fleetwood's office first to confirm my appointment. His assistant tells me she has given Mr. Fleetwood my message and he will return my call once he gets back from vacation. What? Since I've been waiting for over a month to talk to him, I push a little harder. I need to make sure my appointment is on his calendar.

I still don't get a definite answer. And, I feel like I've just been brushed off. Again. She isn't big on customer service. In fact, she's downright rude. Not wanting to argue with her anymore, I strongly suggest she give Mr. Fleetwood my message today. I don't think she heard me. Enough of that office.

Hanging up, I place a call to Jon's attorney, Mr. Jonse. At least his pleasant assistant tells me I can see him tomorrow. Feeling much better about that, I divide my big list into two separate ones. One list for Mr. Fleetwood and one for Mr. Jonse. I feel like I should know Mr. Fleetwood a little more, although I'm not sure why. In reality, I have only met him a couple of times. I remember being in his office once when we originally made our wills, which must have been about

15 years ago. Other than that, we receive a Christmas card from his office. Nothing personal and not even actually signed by anyone.

On the other hand, at least I have an appointment with Mr. Jonse. And, since he knew Jon, I might end up asking him more about Jon. We'll see how I feel tomorrow.

Next, the mail I collected from my neighbor late yesterday is still sitting in the living room. As I sit down on the sofa to go through it, I realize there's not much here. At least, not as much as I thought I would have had. A few bills, credit card promotions, a post card with lions on it from Marissa, a few magazines, and a large, heavy manila envelope addressed to me.

If I didn't know better I would say Jon addressed it. With the same block type he always used, his distinctive printing looked like no one else's. His handwriting was so bad, he printed when he wanted to make sure people could read what he wrote. Hmm . . . other people must do the same thing. I wonder who it's from.

Looking closer, I notice there's no return address and it appears to be stamped San Francisco. But, I don't see an actual postmark or a date on it.

Opening it, several additional envelopes spill out. Each one has a number written on it. Is this a game? Who would send me something like this? After looking at them for a moment, I decide I'll play along. I open the envelope marked #1. It's a letter. Unfolding it . . .

Dearest Stacie,

> *If you are reading this, I must be dead.*

Oh. My. God. Dropping the letter, I blink back tears; tears I thought were done flowing. Apparently I was right when I looked at the neat block printing on the envelope. Trying to stop shaking and to breathe normally, I pick the letter up to continue reading . . .

> *By now, my attorney, Mr. Robert Jonse, will have contacted you and you will realize you are a very wealthy woman. That's the least I could do for you. As everything unfolds, you will understand the much bigger picture of my life. Knowing you, you have questions. Probably lots of questions . . . and probably all written down. That's good. Keep it up.*
>
> *If anyone finds out and asks about your inheritance or why*

I left you a lot of money, please tell them I had invested in some start-up companies. If you mention companies like Apple or Oracle and then tell them I knew when to sell . . . that should quiet most of the rumors.

There will be people along the way to help you through the rough spots. They will offer assistance, provide insight, and help you survive the craziness. Take their advice. Learn from them.

By the same token, there will be other people who will try to hurt you. They may even try to kill you. Stay away from those . . . stay far, far away from those people.

I drop the letter.

15

Who, Jon? Who? How will I know the difference?
Picking the letter back up, I continue on . . .

Talk with my attorney, Mr. Jonse, first. He has other documents for you. They will be ready for you about a month or so after my death. Some of these documents will help answer many of your questions. Do not trust our other attorney, Mr. Fleetwood. He does not have your best interests in mind. It's possible he is no longer around. Things with him were sketchy a few months ago. His office may give you some phony information about him being away on an extended vacation or for business. Don't trust anyone in that office.

Well, that certainly fits with what I have been told by Mr. Fleetwood's assistant. And, I thought he was a family friend. Huh . . .

First of all, I love you. I always loved you and didn't want you to get hurt. I could never tell you the whole truth about my life, however. Now, you will know part of the story. The rest will come to you in a few months. You will understand as this all slowly unfolds.

All what unfolds?

I'm not sure what you were told about my death but it most certainly won't have been the truth. They could have told you I was hit by a car, had a massive heart attack, fell down a rabbit hole . . . who knows? Whatever you were told about how I died . . . it was a lie.

If this package of envelopes has made it to you without being tampered with, I was killed by someone who may have been trying to get back at me or one of my clients.

I know this may be hard for you to grasp right now. I'm so sorry for that. I need you to please keep reading.

At some point, a private investigator, Tom Hansen, will find you. I have no idea how. I just know Tom and I trust him with my life. He knows everything I did. You see, we were partners. He was always the front man.

Tom Hansen? I remember that name from the plane yesterday. What? And, how did he know me?

And what does Jon mean by front man? For that matter, I didn't know Jon had any partners. He was an engineer . . . or at least that's what I thought.

Whatever Tom tells you to do, please do it. No one connects you to me and once I am gone, my clients will have to hire someone else. This business stops when I die. And, that's the part I feel badly about for you. I couldn't tell you what I really did when I was alive. And, now I will never be able to tell you in person. Tom will have to do that for me.

You may have already looked in our safe box in the closet. Please look at it again and pay attention to the bottom of it. Inside there will be a small button to press that will open a false bottom. Please don't be alarmed by its contents.

Oops . . . too late. Already found the box and the secret compartment. Already alarmed by its contents!

The passports were for my other life . . . the one Tom will tell you about. I needed those to be able to perform my job. And, I was good, very good, at what I did. There is one passport with your photo and incorrect information. Don't be spooked. It was just a precaution. I never really thought we would need it, but I had to be safe. Just in case.

Keep those until Tom tells you what to do with them. Don't just throw them away. Make sure they are shredded and then burned at separate times in the fireplace. Throw each batch of ashes away in different garbage cans. Better yet, take a road trip and discard the ashes along the way.

What?

Tom already knows about the gold and will explain. Whatever you do, don't take any of it to a bank. Tom will find a way to get everything exchanged into cash for you.

The handgun is not registered to anyone. It was another precaution I had to take. Tom will explain that, too.

The rest of the letters in this packet should be read in sequence. And, I should warn you . . . you may want a glass of wine as you read through them! Your curiosity will be in its highest gear.

My head is spinning now . . . what more can I read that will make me more curious? I'm probably going to need to read this again. I don't think I absorbed any of this. It's early but maybe wine would help!

Again, I loved you. I was hoping to keep all of this from you.

I have records from all my clients and what they paid me to do. Tom will need access to them and eventually will want to destroy those. I'm not sure, initially, why I kept any paperwork. I guess at the time it seemed easier than throwing them away. They just kept piling up. When encrypted flash drives became available, it seemed like the perfect place to store delicate information. So, anything regarding security is on an encrypted USB flash drive. Tom has that.

You have never seen those files or where they were kept.

More confused, I drop the letter in my lap. So, Jon must have another box with some paperwork in it. Maybe it's in the closet and I just never noticed it before. Picking the letter up I continue on to the next page.

Take a deep breath as you read this last part.

In your office there is a small hidden room . . .

16

W hat the hell?

Go to your bookshelf where all your reference materials and travel books are stacked. I realize you know where every book is, but no one else would ever know it by looking at what appears to be clutter. Sorry about that . . .

One thing you always kept in the same place and always very neat were your favorite photos. Whether they were on the walls or in your files . . . they were organized. I must tell you there was a reason I didn't want to appear in any of those. I couldn't take the chance that someone would put you and me together. Your life would have then been in as much danger as mine.

Huh. No wonder I never . . . never had photos of Jon on any of our trips.

Remove the large photo of the Eiffel Tower at night. The one that hangs next to your book shelf. Now, press hard on the 'nail' that is used to hang it. A narrow door way will open. Don't worry. Nothing will be disturbed and your office will look the same as it always does. The edges of the doorway align perfectly with your shelves.

Putting the letter in my pocket and getting up from the sofa, I head to the back of the house to my office. I really can't believe all this. It's probably just another one of Jon's quirky ideas. I mean, after all, I work in my office. There can't possibly be any doors or walls I didn't know about. Plus, wouldn't I see a door, even if it did line up with my shelves? I am always taking things off my shelves. Goodness, I have a small collection of unusual luggage pieces that I move around from time to time. It's not like I don't pay attention to things in my office. And, I have windows overlooking the bay. Where would another room fit? Or, was this one of the renovations Jon had made before we moved in?

Okay. I'm in my office and I see my favorite Eiffel Tower photo. I took it on one of our first trips to Paris. I love the Eiffel Tower at night. The lights reflect off the Seine and every time I look at this photo, I'm right back in Paris.

Now that I think about it, for a short while I had another photograph hanging there. Jon wanted to hang this one here as he said it was larger and looked better in this space. I wasn't even in the office when he hung it. He said he wanted to use a large nail. So, he asked me to get a larger hammer from his tool box in the garage to do it correctly. He didn't want it to fall down when I was working.

When I got back to my office, he had already hung it. He told me the smaller hammer worked just fine. That didn't even register until now. He must have wanted me out of the room. But, why?

Here goes. No easy task, removing that large of a photo. But, I get it down safely and lean it against my desk. Sure enough, there's a large nail. But, it looks just like any large nail that would hold up any heavy object.

Pressing on the nail, I feel funny. Nothing happens. Am I on Jon's own special candid camera? I press again, harder this time, and then I hear a soft click. Sure enough, a very narrow door way silently appears as that section of my wall swings out towards me. Whoa.

Carefully, I look at my office. Jon was right. Nothing gets disturbed. The edges of the door are cleverly hidden by all my other shelves and books. I'd be hard pressed to find this, even though I now know it's here.

Taking the letter out of my pocket, I continue reading.

17

When you get the door open, there will be a switch near the floor on your right. Flip it. A narrow set of stairs will show up in front of you as the passageway is illuminated. At the same time, the doorway to your office will close.

Yikes.

Don't worry. To get back out, you flip the same switch. The doorway will open and you will be able to return to your office. To close everything back up and leave it the way it was, just press the nail and replace the photo of the Eiffel Tower.

Sure.

Okay . . . Jon wouldn't lead me astray. I flip the switch and in the soft light, I see a small winding staircase that heads upward. Following it up a dozen or so stairs, I come to a small, yet comfortably furnished room. What the heck. I had no idea this was here. Have I really lived in this house for 30 years? When did Jon come up here?

Once I open the heavy shades covering the only window, the view from here is spectacular. Why did I never notice this window from the outside? Maybe it just looks like a fake second story that so many of the homes in this area have. The windows look like windows but aren't real. And, these shades are dark and heavy so no one would be able to see in at all.

The room, no larger than six by six feet, really does look like a tiny yet functional office. A laptop computer sits on a small desk. A small file cabinet flanks one side and a book case sits at the other end. Only, I discover it's not really a book case and they really are not books . . . just made to look like books.

I return my attention back to the letter.

> *I must assume you are in my hidden room. Isn't the view magnificent? I hated to hide this from you, knowing you loved looking out at the Bay. But, I just couldn't chance it.*
>
> *My laptop has very little information stored on it. No one would ever assume it was used for anything except playing games and checking the weather. The file cabinet is locked. You'll find the key on my key ring with my car keys.*

Hmm . . . come to think of it, I never found Jon's car keys. He had that odd key ring in his pocket the night he had the heart attack. Or the supposed heart attack as I'm beginning to think of it. But, it didn't have any keys on it. They have to be here somewhere.

I have my own set of keys for his car. Maybe I should have another look at what's inside his car and the trunk. But, first I need to find the key to unlock this file cabinet. Continuing on with his letter . . .

> *By now you realize the books on the book shelf aren't real. Reach under the second shelf and pull forward on the book with the title "Gone with the Wind". It should open a compartment.*

Yep . . . it sure did. And, I almost fell over.

18

⟡⟡⟡⟡⟡⟡⟡⟡⟡

wo nice, digital cameras, another small handgun, three cell phones, some credit cards with different names on them, more cash, and a bunch of cords, chargers, and various other electrical gadgets are neatly nestled here.

You will see some of my tools. For now, you can leave them all here. Ask Tom what to do with them. He will know how and where to dispose of all of the items. Close everything back up and the room will look like it did when you entered. This is extremely important.

Why? Who's going to find this place, anyway?

The envelope marked #2 will have sheets with all my passwords for all my clients and their projects. It is important that you do not lose that. It is also important that you find a good place to hide it for now. Once Tom reads them, he can destroy them all. Again, trust only Tom and Mr. Jonse. I am very serious about this. I can't stress this enough.

That's all for now. More information will be in the rest of the letters you read. And, Tom will fill you in on other details I may have left out.

Just know these things: 1) nothing has happened the way you thought it has, 2) Tom is your friend, 3) trust Maria in Italy, 4) know that I loved you very much.

That's it for now.

Oh, and make sure you always set the alarm in the house.

Love,

Jon

That's it? That's all? What the hell do you mean? Who is Maria in Italy?

If Jon were here right now, I'd demand more explanations. In fact, I'd probably yell at him . . . something I never did.

But, in all fairness, he did tell me to keep reading the rest of the letters in the packet. Might as well go back down to the living room, pour some wine to have with my lunch, and read until I'm really confused. Won't take much these days.

Wait! Did I just hear something or was that my imagination in overdrive? I could have sworn I heard something fall. It almost sounded like a crash. Quietly, I listen. Hearing nothing, I continue out of Jon's secret room and start down the stairs. I am really spooked now.

But, I am wondering . . . did I set the alarm? I have a habit of forgetting to do that. It's probably why Jon reminded me in his letter. Why is that so important now? As I make my way back down the winding staircase and flip the switch, the narrow doorway opens into my office. Closing the door, I press the nail in the wall and hang my photo of the Eiffel Tower. I turn and look at the wall. It looks just like a normal wall filled with bookshelves, books, and photos. No one would ever know any different.

Amazing . . .

It's then that I hear a series of piercingly loud beeps that quickly turn into one continuous shrilling screech.

19

O ur alarm! I must have set it. That crash I thought I heard must have been someone trying to break into the house. Grabbing my cell phone to call 911, I shut and lock my office door. Instead, my alarm company beats me to it and calls me . . . just like they're supposed to do. I give them our secret code and they tell me the police are on their way.

Two hours later the police are now gone, after they inspected every inch of our house for intruders. They tell me there have been some burglaries in the neighborhood over the last month. Our front door had some scratches on it by the lock . . . similar to other homes close by. And, a planter was tipped over. Probably just kids or small time burglars, they said. No one has reported much, if anything, being taken.

I'm positive everyone I know in this neighborhood has an alarm. Thanks goodness I had remembered to set ours. Never again will I forget to do that.

Everything is safe and secure. Nothing is missing. The police inspected my locks and my alarm. All are in working condition. My mail is still here. I had moved my manila envelope under my books on the coffee table in the living room when I went to my office with Jon's first letter. I'm positive nothing is out of place. Still, I'm squeamish. And even more spooked now.

I look out the windows, halfway expecting to see someone watching the house. Instead, I see nothing out of the ordinary. I double check to make sure my door is locked. But, I can't shake the feeling that someone was watching this whole process. Except, the police didn't find anyone when I mentioned that feeling to them. I'm beginning to scare myself.

Okay . . . I need to refocus, retrieve the envelope, and read some more. Not sure if that will help calm my nerves or just make them worse.

Feet up, I opt for a glass of ice tea with my late lunch instead of wine and settle down on the sofa to read letter #2.

Just like Jon said, it is a series of pages with numbers. I'm thinking the average person wouldn't know these were passwords for clients. Come to think of it, why did Jon have clients that needed passwords? I've already figured out he wasn't the engineer I thought he was. But, the question remains, what kind of clients did he have?

The dates on some of these go back at least 30 years. The whole time we were married . . . possibly before. Looking at one of the earliest dates, I see Florence, Italy, and the year we met. So, he really wasn't on vacation? If he had a client there, why did he need me to show him around the city?

Making sense of dates first, I discover many coincide with my travel assignments. No wonder Jon would disappear for a couple of days while I worked. I'm assuming he would go see his clients.

His clients don't have names, in the sense of real names. Instead, in the first column they appear as two initials, then what looks like a notation for a city, and finally a capital letter. In the second and third columns there are dates. These are usually several months apart . . . sometimes even a year apart. Numbers are written in the next column. These could be phone numbers. Finally, in the last column there is a large number written . . . almost like a dollar amount.

Nothing really looks like a password. At least not a password I am used to looking at. I'm not sure I understand any of these entries. Continuing to look through all of it, I discover a sheet that could be a kind of cheat sheet or legend of some type.

Ahh. Now, I'm beginning to make sense of some of it. Apparently, Jon had his own codes for everything.

The initials are for a person. Not sure they mean anything to me as he doesn't match up those with an actual name. Looking closer, I do see some of the initials are the same, almost as if he worked with that person more than once.

I was right about the city. He means that is the city where he was working. When he writes firenz, he means Florence. Rom means Rome, par means Paris, han means Hanoi. I'm beginning to understand his shorthand for cities. There are dozens of these codes.

He has a guide listed for the capital letter he used. A is for art, G is for gold, W is for weapons, D is for diamonds, J is for jewelry, M is for everything else, whatever that means.

Was Jon a thief?

There is one more page here, folded in half. Written inside . . .

Keep an open mind. Talk to Tom.

20

〰️✦〰️

Huh? Keep an open mind? Talk to Tom?

That's it in this envelope. Remembering Jon's suggestion that I keep this safe, I take the sheets to my office and make two sets of copies. Folding each one into its own envelope, I place one copy in my file labeled 'Italy', the second copy I place under my box of photos with all the other unlabeled envelopes, and Jon's original I place in my carry-on travel purse. My trusty travel purse is always packed and ready for me to travel on assignment at a moment's notice. It sits, waiting in my office, ready to be grabbed for the next trip.

Hopefully, I followed Jon's instructions for the copies. In any case, that will have to do for now. Obviously, I will continue to follow Jon's instructions and ask Tom about all of these.

Thinking of Tom, I need to look for his card and give him a call. I believe it is still right here in my travel purse.

My ringing cell phone takes me back to the living room where I left it. Speak of the devil . . . it's Tom. Did I give him my business card? How did he get my number?

But, of course . . . Jon.

Speaking to Tom, he asks if I have had a chance to read any of

Jon's letters. I find it interesting he knows about them.

Then, he tells me to be sure I read them all before we meet. He says he can meet with me tomorrow. When I tell him about my meeting with Mr. Jonse, Jon's attorney, tomorrow, he says to keep the appointment and that he can meet with me later in the week. He wants to make sure I have read letter #5 and that I talk to Mr. Jonse about it. Tom feels many of my questions will be answered once I meet with Mr. Jonse. After that, we will meet and he will fill me on the rest.

In the meantime, he reminds me again to read all the letters and do anything in them Jon asks me to do. Plus, he stresses for me not to mention any of this to anyone other than Mr. Jonse. When I ask why, he says he is working on that and he will let me know.

I'm mentally exhausted just thinking about all of this. Who were you, Jon?

21

Okay, time to finish my lunch and on to letter #3. It might even be time to open a bottle of wine. I've wanted to try that new Chardonnay from France we discovered a few months ago. This envelope has several sheets of paper in it as well. I'll start with Jon's letter to me, as it's the first page.

Stacie,

Hopefully, you are opening all the envelopes and reading all the letters in the sequence I intended. Knowing you, you are. You are probably a little miffed at me for not telling you any of this. Sorry about that . . . again.

Miffed? Yeah . . . right.

The rest of the notes in this envelope are just that . . . notes. Some are about people we know, some are about people only I knew. Some will shock you and some you won't even care about. Sometimes I will be writing to you and sometimes just making notes of things I want to remember to do. You'll see. Read my notes and keep in mind the context of when and where I wrote them. Afterwards, let Tom read them.

But, once he does read them, make sure they are destroyed.

I'm only giving you these notes as a reference point. I'm just hoping they fit some more pieces of the puzzle together for you. That's what I am trying to do for you.

They are in no particular order but they do have dates that may make some sense for you. Enjoy my scribbles and descriptions. You'll see . . . I'm no writer!

Hmm . . . why would Jon write notes about people we knew? Back to my original question . . . was Jon a thief? If so, why would he need notes on people? Did he steal from our friends? What did he do with the things he stole? Were his 'clients' actually buyers? Is that why he left me so much money?

Enough . . . I really don't want to think of Jon as a thief. But, it's hard not to.

Moving on to the notes, as Jon called them . . . They really aren't in any order and that's odd for Jon. Guess I'll just start reading.

Notes for Stacie on M. R. Fleetwood . . . our attorney. He was referred to me by a so-called friend . . . one that I should have never considered a friend. We need to be careful around Fleetwood. He may or may not have our best interests in mind. Make a note to tell Stacie. He has our wills . . . at least he thinks he does. Need to have no correspondence from him . . . no contact with him. Plus, I'm not sure how he knew Stacie's parents. He asked too many unrelated questions about them. Have to look into that later. And, the wills he has are really of no consequence. Mr. Jonse has those. Note to self . . . Remind Stacie to ask Mr. Jonse about her will.

This is disturbing. I thought we had put our trust in Fleetwood. Jon never said anything to me about him. I wonder what I've said to him or to his assistant since Jon's death. Also, why would he know my parents? They never mentioned his name. He wasn't their attorney. Plus, I didn't realize I had a will at Mr. Jonse's office. I'll make a note to ask about that tomorrow.

Putting that one aside, I move on. Several of Jon's next notes are short and are about people I have never heard of . . . just like Jon said. Skimming these, I'll give them to Tom. They might mean more to him. Picking up the next page, here's a name I recognize . . .

Robert A. Jonse . . . trusted attorney. I must tell Stacie to run any questions or issues through him. I've trusted him for over 30 years. He has the paperwork for all properties, contracts, wills, and deeds. His cell number is as follows . . .

Wait. That number looks familiar. I think it was on that wrinkled scrap of paper Jon had on him when he had his heart attack. Supposed heart attack, that is. The more I look at the number, the more I'm sure it is. The paper was in the plastic bag I put in my travel purse I had with me that day. Going to my office, I find it and retrieve the plastic bag. It still has the paper with the phone number. Sure enough, it's the same number. Why on earth would Jon have his attorney's number on a wrinkled scrap of paper? Why not a business card? And, why would he carry it in his pocket? That makes no sense. Putting the wrinkled paper back in the plastic bag and the plastic bag back in my travel purse, I'll take it with me tomorrow to ask Mr. Jonse. Moving on to the living room and continuing on reading the notes . . .

Tom Hansen . . . my business partner. Like a brother to me. Trust him with my life . . . and Stacie's life. Will take care of unfinished business if I can't. If I'm gone, Tom will take care of letting my clients know. My business ends with my death. Tom will figure out the rest. Must tell Stacie to trust him completely. Keep him in every loop. We've been together since college. Have to find a way to tell Stacie about him.

Wow. Jon really thought a lot of Tom and I didn't even know about him. Since college, huh? Jon never mentioned him. But, he was important to Jon. I wonder what business Jon was talking about. His engineering business? Was Jon really an engineer? Or . . . I'm back to the thief theory.

There is only one more note here. And, it's a long one . . .

Stacie, I need to give you some family history. How I wish I had done this in person.

Peter Sampsoni and Diane Kelly. My parents. They are alive and well. You will recognize Dad's name as a world famous artist and Mom as just as famous a sculptor. But they need to be private . . . very private. As I write this, it seems strange. You probably think so, too. But, it's my life and how I grew up.

Parents!

When I was younger, I was at boarding school in Switzerland. College years were spent at Stanford. The world didn't really know my parents had a son. That's the way they wanted it. Better to be famous and wealthy and not have anyone know you had kids.

Ask Tom to fill in any details I might leave out. I know you loved your family. I loved mine, too. Just in a different way. We could never be in the public eye together. Our rendezvous spot was always the chalet in Austria. No one knew I was actually going there, except for Tom. My plane tickets were for either a ski vacation in Switzerland or scuba diving in Australia. Everything was communicated in our special code.

As you read this, Stacie, keep in mind this was before much of the electronic age we have now. We had to work with what we had.

When I was about six, it dawned on me that my family was different. The nuns at school were used to kids of wealthy parents. I just didn't realize mine were extremely wealthy and extremely famous. Somehow, I knew that the 'uncles' who were always around weren't really uncles or part of our family. Later, I found out they were bodyguards.

My dad had inherited a large family fortune. His dad, Grandpa, owned a large piece of land in Italy around Lake Como and sold it to some future minded developers. He also turned a couple of old palaces in Venice into upscale residences that he sold for quite a profit. I never knew Grandpa. I wish I would have met him. I probably get my sense of buildings and engineering from Grandpa.

Dad didn't follow in his footsteps. Instead, he followed his passion for art. Apparently, he was discovered as a talented artist when he was still in school. The rest is history . . . or so I'm told. Dad's art has sold worldwide, he's been commissioned by some heads of state all over the world, and he owns several art galleries in Rome, London, Milan, Paris, New York, San Francisco, Dubai, and more that I can't remember. That's how he met Mom. She was just becoming a sculptor . . . and after a whirlwind courtship, they were married.

Now, she's famous in her own right.

At some point the whole family fortune thing came to light again and they decided it was better to live a very private life. I grew up in the shadow of this fortune, always mindful not to speak about it. You see, no one except Tom and Maria know they are my parents. And, no one knows how to find them. They are that private.

Now you understand why they gave us the money for our wedding. It's what they wanted to do.

What the hell? I'm having trouble grasping all this. Yes, I recognize the names of Jon's parents. Who wouldn't? But . . . as Jon's parents? I can't seem to wrap my mind around that.

I had no idea. And, why does Jon mention Maria again?

Okay . . . page two of this note.

Let me backtrack for you. I pretty much lived at boarding school, going home only a few times each year. It didn't seem like a hardship or anything out of the ordinary at the time. I had everything I ever needed at school. And, home was a huge place without my friends.

Early on I always knew I wanted to be an engineer and was accepted into Stanford's Civil Engineering Program. I love building things and figuring out how to make structures safer and stronger, so it seemed to be a perfect fit. That's where I met Tom.

Tom and I were cut out of the same mold, only with much different upbringings. He was always smart . . . in fact, smarter than me. I had the resources. While still in college, together we built some of the best prototypes and building designs around. Many of these earned us awards and recognition. We hold patents on many things you might recognize.

Tom's dad was an undercover policeman in the Midwest. When he was killed by drug dealers during a sting operation, Tom decided to join the FBI shortly after graduating from Stanford. As you know . . . or think you know, I did actually join an engineering firm, located right here in San Francisco. I am an engineer. But, I'm more than that.

Especially after Tom came to me with a problem.

22

he FBI was working on an art theft ring . . . involving major works of art.
I will

That's it. The letter stops right here. It's almost as if he was interrupted mid-sentence and never got back to it. There's no more . . .

Now, I am back to Jon being an art thief. But, why? He certainly didn't need the money like I first thought. His family was beyond wealthy.

There are no more notes in this envelope. Placing them back into their envelope, I must remember to let Tom read them. Even though Jon instructed me to destroy them after we were finished reading them, I kind of hate to do that.

This whole process of reading everything is taking longer than I thought. There is so much to grasp as I try to imagine Jon's relationship to everyone. I think I'll fix a quick dinner, have another glass of that wonderful Chardonnay, and look at envelopes #4 and #5. Knowing I have a 10 o'clock appointment with Mr. Jonse in the morning, I need to have all of these read and my questions in order.

Perhaps I should start with the questions that are the most

obvious to me. Specifically: 1. Who was Jon? 2. How did he die? 3. What comes next for me?

Off to the kitchen where I can clear my head while I fix dinner. Then I will continue on with Jon's letters.

Dinner is finished, the kitchen is cleaned up, and I'm settling down on the sofa with my second glass of wine. I open envelope #4.

A single sheet of paper with an address written on it, a key taped to it, and what appears to be a numerical code, falls out. That's it. Nothing else.

Grabbing my tablet computer off the coffee table, I check the address. It's a bank downtown. Not our bank, but one I've heard of. I believe it's close to Mr. Jonse's building, so I could go there either before or after my meeting with him. The key looks like ones used with safe deposit boxes and I bet this is the code for it. I wonder why Jon would need a box in a bank we didn't normally use.

Maybe I'll find more money. Not sure what I'd do with it if I did, though.

Putting the sheet with the number on it and the key in my travel purse, I decide I will go there before my meeting with Mr. Jonse. That way I can add any questions about the contents of the box to my list for Mr. Jonse. I really need to clean out my travel purse but I just haven't had the time to go through it since I returned from Mexico. For now, I'll take it with me tomorrow in case I need to add the contents of Jon's box to it. It has more room than my small bag I usually use when I'm shopping or running errands.

Now, envelope #5. I believe both Jon and Tom said this one was important. It's fatter and heavier than the others. Must have lots of good information in it. I'd better start reading or I'll be up all night.

Opening the envelope, a small note and a cream colored packet with an official gold seal slides out. Everything about this packet screams exclusive and expensive. The weight and feel of the paper are different compared to the others. The raised gold seal with its embossed coat of arms appears genuine. The words 'official' and 'penalty for tampering with' are written in both Italian and in English.

Taken aback, I wonder if I'm tampering with it by opening it. But, Jon told me do it . . . right?

23

---

bviously, this is not something I can just quickly glance at. It's more than a letter and it appears official. It's a good thing it's written in both Italian and English. My Italian is a little rusty.

First the note . . .

Dear Stacie,

This is something I have wanted to share with you for such a long time. I was working out a plan to do that and yet keep you safe at the same time.

You are the proud owner of a villa in Italy. Since we both loved Italy so much, it made sense to have property there. And, since I carry dual citizenship with Austria and the United States, it made it easier for me to purchase property in Italy.

A villa?

This has been in process for several years, but I didn't want to say anything to you until it was finalized. Plus, I was working on that plan to get us both there.

Your villa sits on the lake, is within walking distance to the village, has a boat and its captain for you to use whenever you want, and has a car and driver to take you to and from the airport or wherever you want to go. It has been remodeled with all the best amenities, has a new roof, is completely furnished, and is ready for you to move into whenever you are ready.

There are at least a dozen rooms, maybe more . . . I can't remember. You have your own private wing and there are four guest suites. The spa and surrounding patio have recently been installed. I'm sorry I didn't put in a swimming pool, but I guess you could always do that. That's up to you. Redo anything and everything if you want.

A villa? I still can't comprehend a villa.

Maria, who takes care of everything at the villa, is a permanent resident. She keeps everything in working order and will take care of anything for you. She has her own apartment in one wing of the villa. She means a great deal to me. You'll just have to see it all for yourself. Plus, I can't wait for you to meet Maria. Give her my love.

Maria? That must be the Maria in Italy Jon referred to in one of his earlier letters.

Why does she mean so much to Jon? I'm getting suspicious.

This villa is now yours. It was never in my family, so no one should connect you to me when you are there. You will love it. I know you will. Think of me when you are there. And, if you decide to bring guests, no one will ever know I had anything to do with it. I'd like to keep it that way. It's in your best interest. You can always tell people that you bought it with some investment money.

This is the official deed. It is registered with my attorney in Milan, Mr. Luis Garcia. He will be awaiting your visit. He also has a fund for paying taxes and any special assessments that might come up. Mr. Jonse and Mr. Garcia have been in communication with each other about all of this. Tom knows about this as well.

I must caution you, though.

Don't be too shocked when you see my special, hidden rooms. There are explanations for everything. Tom can fill you in on some of it. Maria will take care of the rest.

And, please tell Peter and Diane hello from me. I really did love them.

I love you, Stacie. I wish I could have told you goodbye in person.
With all my love,
Jon . . .

Peter and Diane? Oh, yeah . . . Jon's parents.

And . . . a villa? With someone named Maria, who probably knows more about my husband than I ever did?

Whoa . . . can it get any more confusing?

Looking more carefully at the deed, I see the attorney's name and phone number in Milan that Jon mentioned. Not familiar with the address of the villa, I guess I will research that next. It appears to be on Lake Garda. And, since I know very little of Italian deeds or property, I should plan a visit once I contact Mr. Garcia.

Looking at the clock and figuring in the time difference, I can't call him quite yet. I'll finish my wine, organize my thoughts for my meeting with Mr. Jonse in the morning, and stay awake until midnight. That way, I can call Italy. In fact, this might be a good time to start on Jon's suits as well. I'm to the point where I can finally deal with donating them.

Oh yeah, I almost forgot. I want to go through Jon's car, too. I'm ready to sell it since I certainly don't need to worry about two cars. I'll put that on Mr. Jonse's list to do as I'm sure he will know how to get that done.

But, I do wonder if there is anything Jon left in his car I should know about. I think I'll go look through it right now so I can let Mr. Jonse know it's ready to go.

On my way to the garage, I catch a glimpse of a moving light outside. Watching it move, it looks like someone carrying a flashlight as the light moves back and forth. It's closer to my neighbor's house than mine but something's not quite right. It's late. My neighbors don't go out and wander around this time of night with a flashlight. Should I call them at this late hour or call the police? Just as I opt to call the police, the light disappears. If I see it again, I'll definitely call the police. For now, I want to look at Jon's car.

24

Many homes in San Francisco do not have garage space for one car, let alone two. Our garage is spacious by those standards. And, like everything else that Jon had his hand in, our garage is well organized and spotless.

It's a good thing I had my own set of keys for Jon's car. I never did find his set. I cannot believe for a minute he lost them. He just didn't lose things.

First, I inspect the trunk. Jon drove a silver Mercedes SLK so I don't have to search a lot of space. There just isn't much space here. Plus, there doesn't seem to be anything unusual here either. After finding hidden rooms and secret compartments, I'm getting wiser about looking at things differently. I always did look beyond the expected . . . just not quite so far beyond.

There is no hidden floor or storage space in the trunk. Thank goodness . . .

The back seat . . . doesn't exist.

In the front, the bucket seats take up most of the room. Jon always said this car barely fit him. It was snug on him . . . but he didn't seem to mind. He loved driving it through the streets and over the hills of San Francisco. But, we rarely drove it when we traveled into wine country, or to Lake Tahoe, or south along the California coast. We always took my car. I never really thought about that until now. Maybe Jon thought his was too small for longer trips.

Searching under both seats, I find nothing. In fact, my hand barely fits there. Unlocking the glove compartment, I find a map of the city and a small dark box. I bring it out into the light of the garage. It's locked. Of course it is. . . .

I'll take it into the house. It seems as if that is the only unusual item in the whole car. Jon's car is in great shape, both inside and out, and I don't think it has a lot of miles on it either. I don't think there will be any problem selling it.

Locking everything back up, I take the box into the kitchen. Since I can't seem to pop it open with a knife and have no idea where the key would be, I'll leave it here on the counter and go to the closet to start on his suits.

25

Opening our closet, I remember how Jon organized his half. We joked about this at the time.

Ahh . . . memories.

Mostly dark colored suits, one might not think there was much difference in their actual color. One would be wrong, according to Jon. There was navy and then there was dark navy. Black was black . . . but with different shading. Gray was, of course, not just gray. And, he did like his suits. He bought expensive ones. And, he kept them immaculate.

Jon wore them well, always looking like they were tailor made just for him . . . which they were. He told me if he was going to spend money on suits, then they were going to fit him. He didn't want them just hanging on him.

Jon's shirts and ties were just as organized. Whites to pastels to off-whites and grays . . . all shirts had their place in the closet. Ties were organized by color and also by stripe, pattern, plain, and then the few whimsical ones.

His dress shoes fit nicely in shoe racks . . . mostly browns and blacks.

Now, everything hung waiting to be worn again. When Jon thought any suit, shirt, or tie didn't look its best, it was given away. Those were not ratty old clothes he gave away . . . they just didn't fit Jon's standards for wearing to work.

As I continue to look through his side of the closet, I see his formal wear. What on earth am I going to do with two tuxedos, two pair of formal dress shoes, and three exquisite white dress shirts? I can't think of any shelter that would want these.

As for my side of the walk-in closet, at least I could say my shoes were well organized. Of course, not by color like Jon's. But, they did line up nicely on their rack. And, I knew where most everything else was. It just wasn't obvious to Jon! I knew what traveled well, so I would grab those things when I needed them. Colors were mixed with black, pants with skirts, dresses usually at the end. It really wasn't important to me where they hung. I just knew what I wanted and reached for it. My formal wear was in a separate section, so I knew where to go to find it. I didn't seem to have a problem finding anything, but Jon loved to tease me about my unorganized, chaotic closet.

Now, once his things are all removed, I will have the whole closet to organize my own way. If Jon could see me now . . .

Okay . . . ties first. There really is no point in keeping any of these. I gave him very few of them, so there isn't much sentimental value there. Folding them up, I divide them into three boxes, one for each shelter. These shelters all have places they work with where men need a decent interviewing suit or ones to wear once they find jobs. They will all go to good use.

Next, the shirts. Again, no point in keeping any of these. Carefully folding them, I divide them as well. Shoes get divided the same way . . . into the three boxes. The closet is emptying out little by little.

Suits are a more time consuming. I really need to go through all the pockets. Jon was famous for tucking little gifts for me into his pockets. Then, when we would be at the symphony or out for dinner, he would delight me with a present. No point in leaving one of those for someone else! I may find something really special. It seems like he made reference to a special gift coming my way soon. Maybe I'll find it!

That would be fun.

But, this could take a while. He has a lot of suits. With a lot of pockets. . . .

26

It's after midnight now but I'm about finished going through countless pockets in what seems like never-ending suits. I'm leaving them on their hangers so they don't wrinkle as I move them to a guest room closet. All three of the shelters will be picking them up in two days.

Reminiscing about places I remember where Jon wore a particular suit has actually helped me as I go through them one by one and remove them from his side of the closet. So far, I've found a pile of 'stuff' that is less than stellar. And, bummer . . . no gifts.

There are credit card receipts from places here in San Francisco that I will shred. Also, a couple of symphony programs, tickets to a ball we attended, seven nail clippers, three other receipts that look like they're in Chinese, and $142. Jon was neat and organized, so I'm kind of surprised I found even this much stuff.

That's it. Except for the tuxedoes. I might as well go through them right now, too, even though I'm not giving those to the shelters. I really don't think they will want those, so I'll find someplace else to donate them. For now, I'll look through the pockets and hang the tuxes and shirts in another closet where I can deal with them later.

Down to the last one, and voila . . . I found a small box from a jewelry store I recognize. Yea . . . I knew it. I just knew it. A present, at last. Holding it to my cheek, I think of Jon and how many times he surprised me with these little gifts. I can't wait to open it.

I'll take it out to the living room to open and offer a toast to Jon with my last glass of wine. Once I look at it, I'll call Mr. Garcia in Milan. It should be after 9 o'clock in the morning there by now.

27

One more glass of wine in hand, I sit on the sofa and stare at the small box. This could be the last thing Jon ever bought for me. It is odd that it wasn't even wrapped, but just taped shut. That's not like Jon. Wrapping was important to him. Well, here goes nothing. What am I going to find?

Removing the tape and lifting the lid, all I see inside is a small key. Not exactly the delightful gift of jewelry I was expecting. Beside the key is a small piece of paper. Picking up the key and turning it over in the light from the end table, it appears to be similar to ones used in jewelry boxes or small cases. It's not very large and certainly not special looking.

Examining the paper closer, I see the word 'registered' written on it. That's it. Turning it over, there's nothing on the back side of the paper.

What does that mean and what is this key? When did Jon become so cryptic? And, why on earth was this in his tuxedo pocket?

Then, out of nowhere comes the thought that I should see if it fits the box from Jon's glove compartment. I left that in the kitchen on the counter. If it doesn't work there, I guess I'll just hang on to it and ask Tom. Seems like I need to have quite the lengthy conversation with Tom.

Somewhat perplexed at what I found and a little disappointed that I didn't find a wonderful gift of jewelry, I put the key back in its small box and set it on the coffee table. Glancing at the clock, I decide to call Mr. Garcia's office in Milan. Then, I really need to get some sleep so I am somewhat coherent in the morning for my meeting with Mr. Jonse. I'll try to open the box later.

28

I'm really glad I took notes when talking to Mr. Garcia last night. Plus, I'm glad I took the time to make my plane reservations. I'm one step closer to visiting my villa!

Reviewing my notes now with my morning coffee, at least some of my questions about the villa were answered. My villa . . . that still sounds strange to my ears. My villa is located on Lake Garda, in Italy.

Jon and I stopped there one time when we were in Venice. Jon wanted to see what it looked like. I knew it was a large lake, but Mr. Garcia filled me in on a few particulars and on a little history. It is Italy's largest lake and probably the most visited with villages and medieval castles, beaches and rocky cliffs. Similar to Lake Tahoe here in California, the water is extremely clear. I do remember Jon was impressed by that.

I would need to fly in and out of Milan and take the train, according to Mr. Garcia. I have no idea why but he gave me a brief history lesson of both Lake Garda and Lake Como. I seem to remember in one of Jon's letters from the manila envelope, he mentioned something about his grandpa owning land around Lake Como. Maybe that's why Mr. Garcia mentioned it.

When Mr. Garcia explained about Lake Garda, he told me there are several towns all around it, with Sirmione probably being the most well known. I do believe that is where Jon and I stayed several years ago. Now, Sirmione caters to tourists and is no longer the sleepy, peaceful town it once was, again according to Mr. Garcia. Tourists have discovered the town, its hot springs, and the Grotte di Catullo.

My villa is actually in another town traditionally called 'Lazise on Lake Garda' or often referred to by the locals as just Lazise. Not being familiar with this town, I will research and learn more about it than what Mr. Garcia told me. He did say it's on the east side of the lake at the foot of the moraine hills. I'll check out the particulars later.

What I did learn, however, that now makes sense, is about the north end of Lake Garda. This area, rimmed with jagged mountains, is known as the Altogarda, and once formed a border between Italy and Austria. Austria . . . where Jon's parents are living. Maybe they've always been from this part of Europe. Maybe Jon came to Lake Garda when he was younger as well.

Finishing my coffee, I glance at the clock and think about leaving early for my meeting with Mr. Jonse. I believe I'm more prepared now that I've read Jon's letters and organized my thoughts.

Oops, I almost forgot. I want to go to the bank downtown first. I have the piece of paper and the key that were in one of the envelopes from Jon. Since the bank is only a few buildings away from Mr. Jonse's office, I can make a quick stop there first.

I'm sure it won't take long to grab what is in the box and turn in the key. There is no need for me to keep a safe deposit box in a bank that I will never go to.

29

S mall bank, but nice. The armed guard at the door checked my identification, entered my name and info into his laptop, and then ushered me inside to the main lobby. I certainly don't remember going through all this at my regular bank. Then again, the bank I usually go to is not downtown. Maybe that's protocol here in the heart of the city. Now that I think about it, I'm really not downtown San Francisco all that much.

As I look around, I realize this is more than just nice. Furnishings are exquisite, almost museum quality, with plush carpet, gold trimmed chairs and tables, and cabinets filled with, what appears to be, crystal stemware. Paintings, worthy of any museum, adorn the walls in every direction I look. Employees are exquisitely attired. Every one of them could be a model. I feel like I've just stepped into a photo shoot for a fashion magazine. In fact, the whole place is so formal that I feel it's quite overdone for a bank. Everyone is pleasant. Nothing appears to be out of order. I'm sure I wouldn't even find a speck of dust if I looked hard enough.

It's probably a good thing I allowed an hour here before my meeting. Ushered into another fabulously decorated, small room off the lobby by an equally fabulously attired woman, I am handed a cup of delicious coffee. I notice no one seems to be rushed. Customer service is at its finest here. I feel special.

Within a few minutes a second fashionably dressed younger lady asks me to follow her to the office of a Mr. Joseph Barth, III. His door plaque reads 'President'. Wow. This is special treatment. Does everyone who comes here get to meet with the president? Now, I am really impressed.

Entering a beautiful ante room and then a huge, overstated office, she directs me to a small sitting area where she introduces me to Mr. Joseph Barth, III. Smiling broadly, he comes toward me and greets me as if he has known me for years. He takes my hands in his and tells me he is sorry for my loss. Well dressed, just like everyone else here, his eyes remind me of a wolf. He's friendly . . . almost too friendly. He continues to hold one of my hands as he leads me to cozy damask covered chairs. I'm slightly uncomfortable with all of his attention.

He says he had known Jon for several years and although he valued him as a customer, he valued him more as a friend. He and Jon were at Stanford together and played tennis both at Stanford and now at their club. He can't believe Jon died of a heart attack. He knew how healthy Jon was. Then, he tells me to call him Joseph. He feels as if he knows me as Jon mentioned me quite often. He asked if I was going to continue writing for the magazines. He waves his other hand in the air as he speaks and I can't help but notice his rings as they shine in the soft light coming through the windows.

Well, no wonder I'm getting the special treatment. He really seems to have known Jon. But, I wonder why Jon never once mentioned him. I thought I knew all of his tennis partners. Plus, I find it hard to believe they were at Stanford together. He seems quite a bit older than Jon. As he talks, my eyes keep catching the light off his sparkly rings. Why would a man wear that many rings?

Joseph continues talking, all the while holding one of my hands in his. He's still waving his other hand in the air . . . it's quite distracting. As I try to graciously remove my hand, he apologizes that he was away on business and was unable to attend the funeral service. When I tell him I really don't remember who was at the service, he tells me he understands. If I need anything, he is glad to help in any way he can. The entire time he is still staring intently at me and smiling broadly. All I can think about are those rings as I wonder how fast I can get out of here.

He goes on to say he hopes I will continue my relationship with him and his bank. He reminds me to call him if I need anything. Once again, he reminds me to call him Joseph. I feel a little smothered by all his attention. Plus, I don't feel like I ever had or even want a relationship with him. He continues to smile at me but I get the sense he is looking straight through me. It's not a genuine smile.

I politely assure him I am trying to get everything in order. I will make all those decisions once I have everything of Jon's organized and all wrapped up. It's been long enough and time for me to move on. He understands that Jon had a lot going on and that it might take me awhile to finalize all of Jon's projects.

Even though I have no idea what projects he's talking about, I make a mental note to make a trip to Jon's office and see about those boxes that were supposed to arrive at the house. Strange I hadn't thought of them until now. Maybe they will offer a clue to Jon's projects.

After some more small talk, Mr. Barth asks if I would like to see the safe room Jon kept at the bank. Somewhat taken aback, I assure him I would. After all, I was expecting a small box . . . not an entire room. But, what the heck. I mean, how big of a room can this small bank possibly have?

Then, he tells me two armed guards will accompany me. Right on cue, they materialize in the doorway.

30

Catching my breath, I stand uneasily. At least he let go of my hand.

But, two armed guards? Is this for real?

Sure enough, the two armed men enter into Mr. Barth's . . . I mean Joseph's office. Both are friendly, in a military stance kind of way. Just looking at them, it's obvious nothing gets past them. They smile, but those smiles don't quite reach their cold steely eyes.

I don't know whether to be alarmed or whether to laugh out loud. What could Jon have possibly put in a room here at the bank that he didn't want at home?

Thanking Joseph, I turn to follow the two guards. Joseph hands me his business card, puts his arm around my shoulders, and tells me to stop by any time. Then, he tells me that everything now belongs to me. *Everything? What everything?* He understands I have an appointment with Mr. Jonse and knows he will confirm everything.

Confused about the room, confused at how Joseph and Mr. Jonse know each other, confused as to what other surprises Jon left for me . . . I smile and head toward the guards who are waiting for me to catch up. Actually, I really want to get away from Joseph. Even though he was Jon's friend, I'm not real comfortable around him. I'm not afraid of him . . . just leery of him. And, I don't want him touching me anymore. He's kind of creepy.

Should I be nervous following two big, burly men into a room when no one knows I even came here? If so, I guess it's too late now. I mean, what else can I do?

There's not a lot that can surprise me at this stage. I think I'm about done being shocked about anything more about Jon. It's apparent he had more than one life. Maybe this room will give me a clue to a life he lived with someone else.

Huh? Hadn't thought about that. Maybe Jon had another wife or even another family. I guess that would be a huge surprise. But, I don't think they would live here in the bank. It must be something else. But, what?

Walking down a short, softly lit hallway, we come to an inconspicuous elevator. Quietly, the door slides open. Motioning me inside, the guards follow and then press a button. The door closes just as silently. I don't see a number on either the button or on the panel, but it does feel as if we're moving. Since it feels like we are going down, I ask one of the guards who confirms we are going down two floors. He tells me this is where the bank has their safe rooms for special customers. When I ask what he means by safe rooms, he looks at me and tells me certain customers want to keep things safe and this is as good a place to do that as he knows about.

Well, that makes perfect sense . . . to somebody. But, not to me. I still don't have a clue what Jon would want to keep safe that he couldn't have kept in the house. We have nice, fairly expensive art hanging on our walls. My jewelry is in our bedroom. Some of our furniture is a little pricey. We have some sculptures by well known artists. What else is there?

The elevator stops with a slight swish and the doors automatically open . . . again quietly. Both guards step out first, glance around, and usher me down another softly lit hallway. They stop me at a richly paneled mahogany door and open a side panel located on the wall next to a door. One guard punches a series of numbers into a keypad and presses his finger tip on a small screen while the other guard looks into what appears to be an eye scanner. They look at each other and nod.

All the while I am standing there watching this, I'm thinking . . . James Bond. A small giggle wants to escape, but I hold it back. These guys are so serious I wouldn't want to upset them. After all, they are armed. . . .

This door opens quietly onto a small foyer. We all enter and the door shuts silently behind us. Once again, numbers are entered onto a keypad partially hidden in the wall. Wondering how many times we are going to do this, that door opens just as quietly as the rest of the doors in this place. I wonder what would happen if just one of these doors accidently made a noise! I probably don't want to know.

Lights come on as we enter what appears to be an elegant storage room. At first glance, a few shelves line one wall, two antique looking chests are against another wall, and a dozen or so heavy looking crates are stacked in the back corner. Plush carpet underneath, three crystal chandeliers hang from the ceiling, and overstuffed, comfortable looking chairs make this more than just an ordinary storage room. Plus, it's quite large. From what I could tell the room is at least 20 feet by 30 feet.

What is this room used for? Does it belong to Jon? Why would Jon need another living room?

I know I must have a puzzled look on my face as one guard tells me I can look around as much as I like. They will wait here for me unless I'd rather be alone. Not sure that I really want to be alone in this closed room, I ask them to please wait. Telling them I just want to get an idea of what is in here, they nod and stand by the door.

I wander around. Opening one of the chests, I discover it's empty. Hoping to find Jon's hiding places for my gifts, I'm disappointed. It's just a nice but empty chest. Turning to one of the shelves I decide to see if anything is there. Again, nothing. This is a nice room . . . but why.

Jon . . . what the hell is this room?

Then I look at the paintings on the wall. A signed Picasso on one wall, a signed Renoir on another wall, and a signed Goya on a third wall. Can these possibly be real? I know a little about art and they certainly appear to be real. If so, they belong in a gallery, not in the basement of a bank. In fact, I thought at least two of them were in a gallery somewhere. What the hell are you doing with these, Jon?

I need to get out of here.

31

Relieved to be back out on the street, heading toward Mr. Jonse's office building, I feel like I'm finally able to breathe normally again.

Maybe I should pinch myself. That was almost unbelievable in the bank. After spending a few more minutes in 'Jon's room' as I am now calling it, the guards brought me back to the first floor where I signed out. Joseph was gone, but I thanked his assistant who told me to come back when I had more time. Right. Why?

Why did I need guards, especially armed ones, to take me to a room two stories below the bank? What was the purpose of all of that? What about those paintings hanging on the walls? Were they real? Everything almost seemed like a staged play or something. And, what did Jon have to do with that room?

I'm still confused and I'm angry that I wasted my time on that unproductive visit. Plus, I had to put up with Joseph Barth and his advances. He gives me the creeps.

This could be a full time job, just chasing after all of Jon's rooms and things. I wonder how many more places like this he has. And, why?

Then it hits me . . . I still have the key and the sheet of paper with the bank's address and series of numbers on it from envelope #4. Strange that no one at the bank even asked me for that. Does it fit another room?

Tom, here's another question I am adding to my growing list for you.

32

Waiting in Mr. Jonse's office area, I take a few minutes to compose myself as I concentrate on the purpose of this meeting. This office is much more welcoming than Mr. Barth's as I glance all around it and eventually out at the Bay Bridge. Mr. Jonse's assistant is friendly yet businesslike. She brought me a cup of coffee as she informed me that Mr. Jonse would be right with me. I'm at ease as I sit and wait.

I definitely want to talk about Jon and I hope Mr. Jonse can fill me in on details regarding his life and his death. After that, I will let Mr. Jonse do the talking.

Welcoming me into his office, Mr. Jonse is cordial yet all business. Not at all like Joseph Barth, Mr. Jonse is professional in his attire and his demeanor. I had only met him once at my house when he went over Jon's will. Yet, I'm quite comfortable around him. He doesn't grab my hand or hug me. And, most of all, he doesn't give me the creeps.

Several packets sit on the table in his office and I can't help but notice Jon's name on all of them. He starts by telling me that everything he knows and everything he will tell me is strictly confidential. If I don't want anyone else to know about any of this, that is my decision. I should know that he will not be giving out any information to anyone but me.

Assuming this is normal attorney-client privileges, I tell him I understand. No small talk here. He tells me he is sure that I have questions and that he may or may not be able to answer them. Again, I tell him I understand. Apparently, I will have the opportunity to ask him those questions when he is finished explaining about the packets. I feel like I'm being lectured by a very nice, yet proper, college professor.

Jon, he tells me, led two very professional lives. No kidding, I thought to myself.

He continues on to say that Jon was most definitely an engineer with a respected firm in San Francisco. Opening the first packet, he gives me documents with pension plan information, stock options from the company, spreadsheets from an investment firm, and a bank statement. Jon had instructed him to take care of all of this in case of his death. Looking at the statement from the bank, the amount of money listed is staggering.

Assuring me this is in addition to the amount he already informed me about, I find myself sitting here looking out at the Bay Bridge trying to catch my breath. He tells me Jon had hired a firm that invested well for him. Combining that with his pension and everything else, it's an amount that will take some time for me to absorb.

Am I ready for the second packet? Sure. What else am I going to say? Maybe we'll get to Jon's second life.

Instead, Mr. Jonse has a whole set of forms for me to sign. Most have to do with taxes and keeping the same investment firm. After glancing at a few, I sign them all. He was Jon's attorney, after all. Jon trusted him. I have no reason not to trust him. Plus, he's a lot more likable and professional than Joseph Barth.

The papers, he tells me, will all be filed with the appropriate entities.

Now, onto the third packet.

It's the title to Jon's car. He tells me I don't need to sell it, but if I want to he can take care of that for me. Thanking him, I tell him of my earlier decision to sell it. It was Jon's. I never drove it and I really see no point in keeping it for sentimental reasons. He agrees and tells me he will handle the details. He will have a service pick it up, probably later today, and let me know when everything is ready for my signature. I nod in agreement.

Looking at me, he asks how I'm doing. He seems genuinely concerned. I tell him I'm doing surprisingly well, that I spent some time in Mexico getting my thoughts in order, and that I am almost finished going through everything of Jon's. I also tell him I have a few questions I'd like to ask when he's finished.

Relaxing a bit, Mr. Jonse pours me some more coffee and says he wants to give me a little history. This might help clear up some of my questions. He and Jon met when Jon was a child as his father was Jon's parents' attorney. After his father died, Mr. Jonse became their attorney and still is to this day. Jon's parents are very well known people. Yet, they have always valued their privacy. For many, many years he has managed all of Jon's parents' affairs, investments, various homes, and businesses.

Okay, things are clearing up a little bit about him. I feel much better about trusting him. I'm still on the fence whether I should tell him about Jon's letters and everything else I've come across.

33

Moving back to business, Mr. Jonse opens the fourth packet, which has only one item in it. It looks like a rather large, bulky address book. Holding it in his hands, he tells me this book is extremely important and that I cannot let it fall into the wrong hands. Continuing on, he says Jon kept it here in his safe, rather than risk someone stealing it.

Steal an address book?

Mr. Jonse explains that he could continue to keep it for me, if I wish. Anytime I need a number or address or any other information from it, we can talk or meet in person. The only times he will give me any information over the phone regarding this book is if I'm using a secure phone.

Telling me that if we go through it together, I might better understand why it is so important to keep this book safe.

Why not?

Handing it over to me, I look questioningly at him. Do I really want to know what's in here? He nods and tells me to look through it. Some of it I will understand and in some areas I will need to get more information from Tom. So, he and Tom know each other?

Arranged just like any address book that I used to use, everything is in alphabetical order. It wasn't that long ago that all of my contacts for magazines were in a book almost like this. However, many of these entries are less straightforward. They appear to be in some sort of code.

Flipping through, I see some names I recognize, but no numbers that I consider to be phone numbers or addresses. There are initials and single digit numbers after most names. Telling Mr. Jonse I don't really get it, he explains that Jon used this book for several reasons.

First, Jon needed private phone numbers for some of his closest friends, partners, clients, and important contacts. He shows me Tom's private numbers and then his own cell phone numbers. That makes sense, now that I know how Jon put them in here. The first quarter of the book has those numbers and contact information. Okay, but why go to all this trouble? There's more here than meets the eye at first glance, he tells me.

The second part lists client's private numbers and what Jon was doing for them. These are all in code, more confusing than the last part. Wrinkling my eyebrows while rubbing my temples, Mr. Jonse can see my frustration. He realizes I know nothing about any of this. When he asks what I know about Jon's clients outside of his engineering work, I stare blankly at him. He tells me to meet with Tom and then, if I decide to leave the book here, I should come back for another look at it. It will all make sense then. But, he wants to make sure I understand it all in the right context.

Finally, he wants to show me the last part of the book. It is not in code but rather a detailed listing of people, a description of each, including notations. He cautions me that I may be shocked to learn something about someone I thought I knew well. These are facts, not someone's opinions. Everything has been verified and re-verified by his law firm. I can take a few minutes to read it or I can come back.

Once again, he strongly urges that I do not leave the office with this book. I agree it needs to be kept in his safe.

34

Trusting my gut instinct, I also trust him more now than when I first met him. I thank him for the fresh cup of coffee that materialized at my elbow and settle in to look at the entries. I will make some mental notes as I look at names and places and then I will leave the book with him to be locked away in his safe.

There doesn't seem to be a particular entry placement about the names. They're not in alphabetical nor numerical order. And, many names I do not recognize. I suppose that's okay. I'm beginning to realize I didn't know much about what Jon did or who his clients were.

Skimming over those names that don't ring any bells with me, I then come to Tom's name. Everything written about him confirms what I read earlier in one of Jon's letters to me. He did graduate from Stanford in engineering and worked with Jon for a couple of years. Then he joined a special department of the FBI. This doesn't tell me much about that. The next entry says that he 'retired' and joined forces with Jon in their consulting business.

What consulting business?

More notes go on to say that Tom was always the contact person. Apparently, Tom referred to Jon by the initials J.J. Wonder why?

Looking up at Mr. Jonse, he tells me I need to ask Tom to fill me in on their business. He will confirm everything and assist me once Tom has given me all the information.

Might as well keep looking through this part of the book. More names I don't recognize, a couple that are familiar to me but I can't quite remember why, and then all of a sudden one name jumps off the page at me.

Mr. M. R. Fleetwood, our family attorney. Or, so I thought until a couple of days ago. I know Jon listed him in one of his previous notes as not being trustworthy. Now, I'm seeing more information about him. I glance at Mr. Jonse and he nods. I keep reading.

It seems Fleetwood is an attorney to several questionable people, including people known to associate with the Italian Mafia. Many years ago a 'so called friend', as Jon writes, insisted he call Fleetwood and employ him as our attorney. Wisely, especially in hindsight, Jon didn't say anything about Mr. Jonse. Jon thought it was best if Fleetwood didn't know of his connection to Mr. Jonse. And, he was right. This 'friend' ended up in some trouble with the FBI and Tom's unit was the one who put him away. It says he died in prison.

Jon apparently had Fleetwood checked out before that happened and questioned some of the reports that came back on him. When he had Mr. Jonse's firm dig deeper, they discovered things about Fleetwood's past, about his clients, and about his interest in Jon. None of this set well with Jon. He didn't want to alarm Fleetwood, so he kept him on as an attorney who had only our basic wills and no access to anything else.

The section on Fleetwood ends with 'DO NOT TRUST HIM'.

Mr. Jonse nods in agreement. Then, he says, rumor has it that Mr. Fleetwood was killed in an accident in southern Italy two months ago. Hmm . . . his office assistant didn't seem to know that. That's odd. Guess I won't worry about keeping any appointments with his office.

Turning the page, one name is written in red ink. DO NOT TRUST immediately follows the name of Joseph Barth, III.

35

What the hell!

I just came from his bank. We talked about Jon, he seemed to know all about Jon and me, he made it sound like he and Jon were great friends, he even had his guards show me Jon's special room . . . I don't understand. Even though he gave me the creeps, I didn't really have any specific reason not to trust him.

Mouth hanging open, I stare at Mr. Jonse with a bewildered look on my face. He can tell I am really confused.

He refills my coffee, adds some sugar, and tells me to take a deep breath. He is going to fill me in on Joseph Barth, III once I read Jon's entry about him.

According to Jon, Joseph Barth, III did attend Stanford. But, not at the same time. Occasionally, they now played tennis at the same club . . . but not as partners and didn't see each other nearly as often as Joseph made it sound. The bank where Joseph is president was owned by Joseph's grandfather, who made his money in the logging industry. Joseph's father inherited that wealth and wanted all the finer things that his business associates had. The problem was, those associates had had their money for generations. They knew how to act. Joseph's father just accumulated his wealth relatively recently. He didn't work for it. And, he didn't know how to use it.

Joseph's father tried to buy his way into certain clubs, he paid beautiful women to accompany him, he wore gaudy, expensive jewelry, and when he couldn't buy what he wanted . . . he found a way to steal it. Most of the time, he paid someone else to steal it for him. But, one time he wanted in on the action and it backfired. He and his thieves were caught in the act and ended up either killing each other or committing suicide. He's not clear on the details. I should ask Tom about that.

Bottom line . . . Joseph Barth, III inherited a bunch of money . . . and all of his father's bad habits.

36

---

ortified with another sip of coffee, I keep reading.
Jon adds that Joseph now owns the bank.

> *WARNING . . . before you go to his bank with my key
> and pass code to my safe deposit box, talk to Mr. Jonse. He will
> have someone accompany you to the bank and stay with you
> while you empty out the contents of that box. Then you can
> turn in the key and have nothing more to do with Joseph Barth,
> III or his bank. There is a reason I had the safe deposit box in
> his bank.*

What? What about the room I was taken to? What about the
armed guards?

When I question Mr. Jonse, he tells me he thinks Jon explained
some of it and to keep reading. Sure enough . . . Jon continues on.

> *Please don't go to the bank alone. Barth is a womanizer, a
> snake, a thief, and not to be trusted with any information he
> will try to weasel out of you.*

Oops . . . too late. I already discovered some of that.

> *Barth may try to take you to a room in the basement. He
> may even try to tell you it is mine. It's not. He holds his secret*

meetings there and tries to impress people. Don't believe a word he tells you. Don't spend too much time looking around and don't question him about the artwork on the walls, either. Do not give him any information about our lives, your inheritance, your plans, and most specifically, do not mention Tom to him.

Ask Mr. Jonse to tell you more about him.

That's it. That's all Jon wrote.

Closing the book, I look at Mr. Jonse with questions written all over my face.

Patiently, he fills me in on Joseph Barth, III. Joseph, he begins, has been under investigation by the FBI and the Banking Commission for over a year. This is a secret on-going investigation that may come to an end in the next month or so. Tom has not been directly involved, but his former unit is in charge of the investigation. Tom has been giving information to the unit via Jon and others. Bottom line . . . it has to do with stealing and smuggling.

Stealing? Smuggling? Why would Jon know anything about smuggling?

Before Mr. Jonse continues, I tell him since I had Jon's note with the key and numbers and since I was downtown, I went to the bank before I came here. Definitely surprised by this, he asks me to tell him what happened. I go through the whole episode from start to finish, leaving nothing out. I include telling him my feelings about Joseph, how he kept leering at me, and that Joseph knew I had an appointment here next. How did he know that?

Slightly perplexed, Mr. Jonse tells me he'll figure that out. He finds it strange that Barth's guards would take me to the room downstairs. Apparently, he wanted to impress me by proving he and Jon were really good friends. He is glad I had not mentioned my key and numbers from Jon to Barth. Once we are finished here, he will go with me to the bank and we can be done with Barth, once and for all.

It's better if I have nothing to do with that creep after I see what Jon has in the safe deposit box.

37

My head is spinning as I hand the book back to Mr. Jonse. He reminds me I can contact him or stop by anytime if I need to check on a name or just have something I want to look up.

Sliding the last packet on his table over to me, he assumes I already know what is in it. It is all the paperwork for my villa in Italy. He knows Jon left me a copy of the deed and gave me Mr. Garcia's number in Milan. Telling him I have already talked to Mr. Garcia, he is pleased and asks me when I plan on making the trip to see my new property. I tell him I just made reservations last night and leave in four days.

As it turns out, Mr. Jonse and Mr. Garcia know each other from some previous property acquisitions for Peter and Diane. Mr. Jonse has not seen my villa but has been to visit Jon's parents in Austria.

Mr. Jonse asks me if I have met Peter and Diane, Jon's parents, yet. When I tell him I really didn't even know who they were until recently, he tells me he understands. Then, he suggests I make an effort to contact them. I start to tell him I have no idea how to do that, and he says he will help me. He tells me I can ask more questions as soon as he fills me in.

Since it's well into lunch time, he suggests we order lunch and go over any remaining questions I have here in his office. I'm good with that.

He starts at the beginning . . . Like he mentioned earlier, his father was Jon's parents' attorney. He was more than that, though. He helped Peter get started in the art gallery business. Peter, he tells me with great pride in his voice, is the artist of the century. At one time he had no interest in selling his work. He'd rather paint. Mr. Jonse's father encouraged Peter to buy a gallery in Switzerland just so he could display his artwork. Then, he would have more room at home to paint.

One gallery led to another one in London, then one in Milan, and then one in Venice. And, his paintings were not just being displayed. They were selling. For a lot of money. Soon afterward, Peter met Diane, who was becoming known as a sculptor, and they were married after a short engagement. Jon was born 10 months later.

By now, Peter and Diane had a couple of homes in Europe and galleries in several more cities. They tried to maintain a private lifestyle but sometimes it was just impossible. When Jon was five, there was a threat on the life of Jon's nanny. But, since they didn't know if the nanny or Jon was the real target, they decided it was time to pay more attention to everything around them. They hired Mr. Jonse's father as a full time attorney to run their affairs and hired more private security for them. A year later, Jon started going to boarding schools, seeing his parents only at holidays.

That's also when he, Mr. Jonse, first met Peter, Diane, and Jon. Jon always said he wanted to go to college, become an engineer, and build things. Mr. Jonse was already following in his father's footsteps, had graduated from law school, and was well on his way to becoming a successful attorney in San Francisco.

They kept track of each other and when a year out of college Jon settled in San Francisco, he looked up Mr. Jonse. He hired him to take care of all his work, his contracts, and oversee his investments.

Looking me squarely in the face, Mr. Jonse tells me several things. First, I do need an attorney. He will be glad to recommend one if I decide not to continue on with his firm. He says I can call him anytime on his private line and he will help me with whatever I need. Plus, he knows I've been given a lot of information in this short amount of time with him. Anytime I want to come back for more explanations, clarification on anything, or to get other questions answered, I just need to call his assistant to set up a meeting.

Next, he suggests I contact Jon's parents with the numbers he will give me. He assures me they are awaiting my call and want to meet with me. They know Jon is dead and feel bad they haven't yet met me.

He tells me to pay attention to what Jon has told me, to what Tom will tell me, and to my gut instinct. If something or someone doesn't feel right . . . then follow that instinct. It will keep me safe.

He urges me to inspect the villa in Italy, paying close attention to what Maria has to show me and tell me.

Finally, he asks if I'm ready to find out what is in Jon's safe box at the bank.

38

I'm positive my head is actually spinning. So much information. So many more questions. But, I know I will sort them all out.

Mr. Jonse and I leave his office and head back to the bank I now refer to as Mr. Barth's bank. The same guard greets us at the door and enters our information into his laptop once more. He tells me it's nice to see me again. I offer a lame smile.

Once inside, the same well dressed lady greets us and assures us that Mr. Barth will see us shortly as he is in a meeting right now. Mr. Jonse tells her that won't be necessary as we are only here to remove some contents from a safe deposit box and then close that account. She insists Mr. Barth will want to see us. Mr. Jonse is more persistent and almost demands we be taken to the room where the safe deposit boxes are kept.

After what seems like a tug of war, she relents but sternly tells Mr. Jonse he will NOT be allowed in the room with me. Apparently, only the holder of the key is allowed inside. She will usher him to another room, clear across the foyer from the room where I will be.

I'm beginning to panic a little as I don't want to be in any room in this bank by myself and he can see it in my face. He suggests either I let him access the box or that he wait close by. Nodding, I agree. I want him right outside the door to the room with the safe deposit boxes.

Mr. Jonse explains to the woman that he will be waiting there, immediately outside the door, as I have not been feeling well today and I might need his assistance. At first, she tells him she cannot break protocol. Finally, seeing the stern look on his face, she can tell he means it. Mr. Jonse is allowed to stand next to the locked door.

I am ushered into a small room with a desk and two chairs. A thought runs through my mind. If only one person is allowed in here, why two chairs? Unlocking a second room, she first looks at the number on my key and directs me to the wall where my box is located. Entering her key, she instructs me to do the same. Turning them simultaneously, the outside door to the box opens.

Pulling out a rather sturdy box, she helps me set it on the table. She tells me I am to enter my special number once she is out of the room. That will open the box for me.

Thanking her, I glance up as the door softly closes behind her. I am alone with Jon's box. It's not huge; probably 18 inches long by 10 inches wide and four or five inches high.

Thinking it's now or never, I enter the code. A loud click seems out of character in this place where everything is so quiet and soft. Opening the lid, I see only one item inside.

A black velvet case, embossed with the imprint of a world famous jeweler, stares up at me. Lifting it out, I feel around inside the rest of the box. Nothing else is here.

I'm pretty much done hoping to find any gifts of jewelry, but it sure does look like a box that would hold a nice piece. I just hope it's not another key or another clue. I'm tired of clues. Taking a deep breath, I tell myself it's time to see what this is.

Flipping open the little gold latch, I lift the lid. I'm staring face to face at the most magnificent diamond and emerald necklace I have ever seen.

I try to shut my mouth.

39

Quickly closing the lid to the jewelry case and latching it, I look around. Is someone watching me? It certainly feels like it. Why do I have a chill running down my spine? Why do I feel funny? I'm positive my hair is actually standing up on the back of my neck and once again I have the distinct feeling I am not alone.

Glad I decided to bring my larger travel purse with me instead of my usual small clutch bag, I remove most everything from it and carefully place the black velvet box at the bottom. Then I put my other things back on top. Not sure why I'm being so careful, it just seems like the right thing to do. I double check the safe deposit box and once again find nothing else in it. A giggle escapes . . . why would I expect something else?

Opening both doors, I find Mr. Jonse waiting for me right where I left him. Sitting at her desk across the large foyer is the lady who helped us. She does not appear as happy as when we first entered. I turn in my key and ask for a receipt. I want nothing else to do with this place. Still insistent that Mr. Barth will want to see us, we patiently tell her we have other appointments and that we need to go. I thank her for her assistance and we immediately make a beeline toward the door.

Damn! Down the hall from the right comes Mr. Barth, who calls my name. Since it would be awkward and rude to make a run for the door, we stop to chat. He takes my hand and instead of shaking it, he gives me a hug. Totally unprofessional, if you ask me. As his hand brushes my purse, it starts to slip off my shoulder. He grabs for it but Mr. Jonse is closer and much quicker. He retrieves it before it falls all the way off my shoulder, gives it back to me, and I tuck it under my other arm. I may be reading too much into his expression, but Mr. Barth looks upset. Very upset.

Mr. Jonse explains we have other appointments to keep and politely tells him good bye. I just nod and move away from him. Before we are more than a couple of feet away, Mr. Barth calls my name and tells me that I must come back and visit him again. Better yet, he says, he will invite me to dinner so we can talk about Jon.

Right . . . that's not going to happen, I think to myself. I could have sworn I heard the ever proper Mr. Jonse chuckle.

40

We don't speak on the way back to Mr. Jonse's office. I'm still a little upset and somewhat bewildered. Once safely back in his private office, I reach in my purse and take out the black case. Before I open it, I ask him if he thinks Jon has done anything wrong. Then, I ask him if he thought Mr. Barth wanted to see what was in my purse or if he just accidentally bumped it off my shoulder.

Telling me, with total certainty, that everything Jon did was legal and appropriate, I am relieved. He does offer a 'however' to that statement, though. Sometimes Jon had to work in a gray area. And, often he was working around unsavory people.

As an engineer or as something else? Not to worry, Tom will fill me in . . .

As for Mr. Barth, Mr. Jonse wouldn't put it past him to try to dump out my purse so he could see what Jon kept in the safe deposit box. Not for a moment does he think it was accidental. I didn't think so, either.

Unlatching the black case, I turn it so Mr. Jonse can see the contents. Carefully he lifts the necklace out and holds it up to the light. It sparkles as light from the window dances off of it. Even though I am positive, I still ask him if he thinks it is real. He tells me he knows it is, as he knows where it originally came from.

Seeing my quizzical look, he explains. Some wealthy woman, probably a duchess or a countess, was given this necklace, a matching bracelet, and a 10 carat emerald solitaire by her husband in the early 1900s. It was passed down through the family, and ended up belonging to a granddaughter of the original owner. One night in the 1960s, at a fundraising gala in Paris, the granddaughter was wearing all of her grandmother's magnificent jewels. Apparently, all the women there were decked out in their finest jewelry. That evening many of them put their jewels in the hotel safe.

When the safe was opened late the next morning, all the jewels were cleaned out. No one ever found the thief or the jewels. Fast forward several years to about 1990 and what appeared to be the same necklace, but only the necklace, was spotted on another woman here in San Francisco. It was rumored she was a descendant of a long line of jewel thieves.

She was also linked to the hotel manager or concierge where the theft occurred. The story gets confusing. Coincidence? Probably not.

The family of the original owners wanted the pieces back. You can see why. Not only are the stones and setting exquisite, but it's a family heirloom. A reward was offered. A 'no questions asked' reward. The family wanted it back where it belonged.

It was also noted that the woman wearing it had ties to important people here in the city. The news was splashed all over the papers in Europe and here in San Francisco as well. It was quite the scandal. Then . . . nothing. Mr. Jonse tells me he wasn't sure what happened to the necklace, the rest of the set of jewelry, the lady, or the story. She and the necklace seemed to have vanished. Apparently, the bracelet and ring have never surfaced.

But, Tom knew about it. In fact, Tom was the one who discovered who the woman was related to. So, now it's come full circle.

The woman who was wearing the necklace in San Francisco was the sister of Joseph Barth, III.

41

tunned, I stare at Mr. Jonse. How can this be? Was she arrested? How did Jon get it? How do we get it back to the owners? Better yet, did Joseph Barth know this was in his bank all along?

Mr. Jonse continues on with more of the story for me. After Tom's investigation turned up the truth about her, she supposedly committed suicide and the necklace seemed to disappear once more. Mr. Jonse had suspicions that Jon and Tom might have been involved. They never told him. That's okay . . . it's just the way it works.

He isn't sure if Joseph Barth, III knew it was in his bank all this time. Mr. Jonse suspects Barth did know it, but has no proof of that. I tell him about the feeling I had in the room with the safe deposit boxes, where it felt like I was being watched. He tells me he wouldn't put it past Barth to do that.

Barth watching me? Yuck . . .

As for getting the necklace back to the owners, Tom will take care of that. It was his investigative unit that found it so it makes sense to have him return it. There will most likely be a reward but he doesn't think the family will make a big deal of it. They don't like the paparazzi dredging up old scandals.

Discreetly, Mr. Jonse's assistant enters and hands him a note.

After reading it, he explains to me that Tom will not be able to meet with me at my home. He has been called away. But, he plans to meet me at my villa in Italy in one week.

When I ask him what I should do with the necklace, he tells me I can either leave it here in his safe and he will give me a certified receipt for it or I can take it to my own bank and put it in a safe deposit box there. By now, I trust him completely so I tell him I will leave it here. He can let Tom know it is here. Besides, I would feel very conspicuous walking around the city with this in my purse. I know jewelry and this is one expensive piece.

I tell him Jon left several letters and things for me that I need answers to. But, when I ask him what more he can answer for me, he stops me and says that I need to talk to Tom first. Then, he will be glad to fill in any remaining details that he can. I guess I'll have to be content with that until I meet with Tom in a week.

Admiring the necklace one last time while he writes me a receipt, I can't help but wish it could talk to me. I would love to know about the original owner, its history, who has worn it, and where it's been in between being stolen in Paris and ending up here, in San Francisco. What a travel piece that would be.

Just a few last details, he tells me. He reminds me to call Jon's parents before I leave for Italy. They will arrange for us to meet. Next, he tells me that anything Jon left for me, I need to make sure I follow his instructions. If any handguns are included in that, I should tell no one, other than Tom. He will take care of them for me.

Mr. Jonse then reminds me that Jon's car will be picked up no later than tomorrow and I can sign any documents at that time. The money will be deposited wherever I decide.

Reminding me to set my house alarm, he tells me it might be a good idea to let my neighbors and the city police know I am going to be gone for a few weeks. He asks if I have noticed anything out of the ordinary around my home. When I tell him I thought I saw someone with a flashlight walking around outside last night, he tells me to be aware of all things like that which don't make sense. Remember to follow my gut instinct, he tells me.

Then, he says that if anyone other than Jon's parents or Tom contacts me, I should immediately notify him. He asks for my cell phone and enters his private cell phone number into my contacts but he doesn't use his real name. He uses the name of Elmer. Looking at him questioningly, he smiles and says Elmer was his first dog's name.

He was a bulldog.

42

Since I am only about four blocks from Jon's office, I decide to make a quick stop and inquire about his boxes. I can have them brought to the house before I go to Italy. I'm already parked in the private ramp for this building so I will just leave my car here for a little while longer.

Jon's assistant, Shelly, greets me and tells me she is so sorry for my loss. Jon was such a joy to work with. I've always liked Shelly and I feel badly I haven't talked to her more. When I apologize for not picking up Jon's things much earlier, she tells me they have been boxed up and awaiting my okay. A moving service can deliver them to my house this afternoon. I tell her I didn't remember that Jon had that many things in his office. She explains that he had several offices in the building. Some offices were for his current architectural drawings, some for storing old documents, one for his day-to-day working, and one with scale models in it. His items were all carefully boxed by her, as she knew how important they were to Jon's work.

Shelly goes on to tell me that there is a spreadsheet on his laptop with his former client's names and numbers, in case I should need to get in touch with any of them. Since she understood how particular Jon was about his equipment, she was the one who packed up his laptop and his electronic gear. There was no way she was going to let a moving service do any packing. They're great at moving but she thinks she's much better at packing. She's seen how they work and doesn't think much of that. Then, she hands me an envelope that includes passwords for all of Jon's devices. This was an envelope Jon entrusted to her and she has never had the need to open it.

We chat a little while longer and I find out she is now working for another engineer in the building. He's okay but not as neat as Jon.

As I thank her once more and turn to leave, she tells me to tell Tom hello. She hasn't seen him in a couple of months. And, then she says she almost forgot about the key.

Another key?

Unlocking a small box beneath her desk, she hands me another small envelope. Inside, she says, is a key to the unique looking case that was in one of Jon's offices. That case is with the rest of the things that the moving service will be bringing to me later today.

She always liked the look of that case. But, in all the years she worked for Jon, she never unlocked it. Jon told her to give it to me if anything ever happened to him. She had a feeling it was private. But, she also has a feeling that Tom knows about it. And, she says it's kind of a cool looking case.

More luggage for my collection, I think as I head back to my car.

43

Whew! What a day, I think as I arrive back home. Has it really only been one day? I've learned so much and I still have so much to learn. It seems like I've accomplished so much and yet still have so much to do.

One of the first things I need to do is to contact Jon's parents before I leave for Italy. Then, I need to let the neighbors and the police know I will be gone, I need to figure out what to do with the boxes from Jon's office, and . . .

Almost as if on cue, my doorbell rings. It's the moving service with the boxes. Good timing. Since there are not as many as I feared, I have them bring the dozen or so boxes into the dining room. Everything is labeled. Shelly did a great job on that. I have the movers stack them according to the room numbers listed on the boxes to make it easier for me once I have time to go through all of them.

After they leave, the only one I really want to find is the box that has the unique looking case in it. The one the key fits. Shelly told me it would be in one of the boxes from Jon's main office, labeled Room #1. Okay, that narrows it down to one of four of the boxes. The first two are boxes of electronics, cables, a laptop computer, and what appears to be laptop or other device chargers of some type. Another box is full of notebooks, engineering books, and calendars. So, that locked case must be in the last box labeled Room #1.

Sure enough. When I open the last box I see a non-descript, brown, leather looking case with a handle. It's not overly heavy as I lift it out. And, it's about the size of a small, squatty briefcase. All in all it's about 18 inches long, eight inches wide, and 12 inches tall. But, it is locked. And, Shelly was right. It's a cool looking case.

After all the things I've witnessed today, like the surprise in the safe deposit box, the confusing room, and the overly aggressive Joseph Barth, III, all from the bank . . . this seems just like a harmless chapter in a puzzle book. Picking up the case, I head to the kitchen where I will open it while drinking a nice glass of dry Riesling wine. After all, it truly is five o'clock somewhere . . . in fact, right here in my kitchen. Plus, judging by the looks of this case, it probably has more engineering stuff in it. Things Jon might have needed in the field. I can't imagine I would find another handgun. That would be just too bizarre.

Once this one is inspected, I will grab the box from Jon's car and see if the key from his tuxedo opens it. That way, I think I'll have looked in all of his boxes. It sure seems like Jon loved small boxes and keys.

Unlocking this case, I open the lid, which makes the whole thing unfold sort of like an old fashioned train case. As the top opens up fully, two small shelves raise up, one on the right side and one on the left. Each of those shelves has another small dark grey box sitting on it. Fascinated by the workings of the case, I wonder where Jon found such a unique piece of luggage. Because, that's what it looks like as I inspect it closer. Old time luggage. Funny that he never showed it to me before. He knew how I loved unusual luggage. I will definitely add this to my collection in my office.

In the light of the kitchen I can see into the bottom of the case, where another small box sits. I take that out and it sits comfortably in the palm of my hand, with its shiny blue-green, lapis-looking cover, gleaming up at me. Wow! This is gorgeous. I wonder if it really is lapis. I know I've seen lapis but I don't know enough to know whether this is real or just made to look like the real thing. Whatever it is, the workmanship is beautiful.

I wonder why Jon would have this gorgeous little box in this case and why on earth he would store in his office. Then it hits me . . . maybe this is my special gift he mentioned.

44

Running my fingers over the smooth top, I admire it, regardless whether it is real lapis or not. Inspecting it a little closer in the light, I think it is real lapis. I'll take it to our jeweler to make sure, though. Turning the box around, I see the rest of the box appears to be sterling silver. Sure enough, the bottom is stamped with the familiar .925 telling me it is.

Then I notice the small latch. Hmm . . . it's not just the decorative box I thought it was. It's an actual case for something. Now, I'm really intrigued.

Carefully, I release the tiny latch and the top opens smoothly. Inside, nestled in the dark black velvet lining, rests a ring. Wow! Not just any ring, but a square cut emerald flanked by two smaller square cut diamonds. Staring at it for several seconds, I finally close my mouth and remove the ring. Not gaudy, not overly huge . . . it's elegant. That's the only word that comes to mind as I look more closely at it in the light. Elegant.

As I slip it in on my finger, it fits perfectly. It's as if it was made just for me.

Jon knew I loved all jewels. But, he knew I really loved emeralds and diamonds. This must be what he was going to give me as an anniversary gift. This is special . . . really special.

I pour another glass of wine, raise it in a toast to Jon and our wonderful years together, and admire the ring on my finger. Thanks, Jon. Tears form in my eyes.

I had been wondering if I should wear my wedding ring on my right hand. I don't know what the protocol is for that. I'm certainly not going to leave it at home. Jon gave me that one 30 years ago and now I have this wonderful ring he also gave to me. Perhaps I will wear this one in place of my wedding ring. I could ask our jeweler about the proper place to wear my wedding ring, a stunning three carat solitaire set in platinum. It would look okay on my right hand.

Enough thinking about ring protocol.

Perhaps I should look through the rest of the case before I put it in my office. I won't travel with it, but it will be an interesting piece to display with my other travel gear. It's so unique. I'd still like to know where Jon came up with the case. It probably qualifies as an antique.

Still wearing my new ring, I make sure nothing else is in the bottom. Then I look at the two shelves that opened on the sides. They each contain a flat, dark gray velvet box.

45

No longer worried that I might find another handgun or cryptic note, I'm ready to see what surprises these hold. After all, these look just like the cases our jeweler uses. I think I've finally discovered Jon's hiding place for my gifts. No wonder I could never find anything in the house. He kept them at his office. Sneaky guy!

I know we were going to be married 30 years, but the ring would surely have been enough of a gift. Maybe he was keeping these for Christmas or my birthday. Let's see what they are. I can always give them to myself later. Yeah, right.

Opening the first case, a necklace to match my new ring sits and smiles up at me. Again, not gaudy or overstated. It's a simple, yet elegant piece. After seeing the one earlier today, this one is more my style. Admiring it on me as I walk to look at myself in the hall mirror, I think that Jon knew me so well. And, I love him for that.

So, what am I going to find in the other case? I mean, what else could match up to these pieces? Possibly a bracelet? Probably not. Jon knew I didn't wear many bracelets. But, I was always surprised by him. Time to find out.

The second case holds another necklace, an unusual necklace. It's a white gold chain with a small but sturdy looking key on it. Okay, now we're back to cryptic. That's it. Nothing else. I don't get it. It's not like Jon to give me 'the key to his heart'. He wasn't sentimental like that.

Checking out the luggage case, there is nothing else in it. Maybe Tom or Mr. Jonse will know the meaning of this key.

Speaking of keys, I need to retrieve the one from Jon's tux and see if it opens the box from his car. I'll do that right after I fix dinner.

46

Settling down in the living room with the box from Jon's car, the key from his tuxedo, and the attached note, I really don't think I can possibly find more jewelry. Can I?

And what does Jon mean by this short note? All it says is 'it's registered'. Time to find out.

The key does indeed open the box I found in Jon's car. And, once more I'm surprised by the contents of yet another one of Jon's boxes. Another small handgun sits and stares up at me. Included is an envelope with my full name written on it. Opening the envelope I find the purchase receipt dated almost six months ago and a business card from the seller. It appears that it is registered to me. Hmm . . . why on earth would Jon buy me a handgun and not tell me about it? Why would he keep it for so long in his car? I don't even know how to shoot. I don't even know what kind of handgun this is.

I will definitely ask Tom about this. I wonder if I should call the seller tomorrow to see if he knows anything about it. Possibly, if I have time. There is so much to do before I leave for Italy in four days. It was amazing I was able to get such great tickets on such short notice.

I need to contact the magazine and let them know I probably won't be able to make it to Venice for the America's Cup trials. Without revealing my exact plans to them, I will tell them I could do other features for them in Italy, however.

Then, I still need to contact Jon's parents in Austria. With the time difference I could stay up a little later and do that tonight. That will be quite the conversation. I have no idea what Jon told them about me. For that matter, I really have no idea what to say to them. I hope they speak English. My Italian is a little rusty and my Austrian non-existent. Or maybe they speak German. I could order a beer in German, but that's about the extent of my language skills there. Should be interesting to say the least.

I will let my neighbors and the police know I am going to be gone for about three weeks. And, I need to leave a message for Tom as to my plans and when I will be at my Italian villa. My villa . . . I still can't get used to saying that.

Next, I need to update my list of questions for Tom. That list is growing by the hour, it seems. I guess I could do that on the plane.

I need to put this case with my handgun somewhere safe in the house. It will probably go in my office files or in the secret room I found. I can ask Tom what I should do about it.

Usually, I don't travel with much jewelry, but I might make an exception this time. I could wear these two new pieces. No one would see the necklace if I keep it under my sweater. It just seems right to have it with me.

And, I still need to pack.

Do you suppose it's too early to call Austria?

First, I head to my office to put everything safely away. Then, I check my computer for messages and to see what the weather is like in Italy. I figure I'll be gone for about three or four weeks and don't want to over pack.

Since I don't look out my window to the side street, I don't see the black car by the curb.

47

Finally, settled in first class on my way to Milan by way of Zurich, I can't wait to see my villa. I'll spend a couple of nights in Milan, visiting with Mr. Garcia. He assures me my driver will meet me at the airport and bring me to Mr. Garcia's office. Then my driver will take me to Lazise once Mr. Garcia has filled me in on everything I need to know or do. I won't need to take the train this time. Even with all the odd events of the past week, it seems like a dream to actually be on my way.

I haven't given much thought to what I will do once I am in my villa. It still doesn't seem quite real to me. I know I meet with Tom in three or four days as he left another message for me. And, I get to meet Maria. Believe me; I have all sorts of questions for her, too.

The phone call with Jon's parents wasn't nearly as strained as I thought it might be. Of course they spoke English and they seemed so nice. They will visit me at the villa in a few days. I offered to come to Austria but they insisted I could do that once they see the place Jon picked out. It seems that they hadn't seen it yet, either.

So, I guess most of my time I will be entertaining guests as I find my own way around. I have the list I condensed for Tom. By putting it into categories and leaving blanks from Mr. Jonse's information, I think I can get a better idea of what Jon did as what appears to be his second career. I'm no longer thinking of him as a thief, but more of a consultant to whatever it is Tom now does. And, I know Jon really was an engineer. I looked through more of his boxes from his office.

Drawings, models, and addresses of the buildings he had worked on were mostly all familiar to me. Although, one of the notebooks had notations similar to those on one of the spreadsheets Jon had in the large packet. I still don't quite get the abbreviations though. The rest of his addresses are so plainly written. Why would he have some in code? That is definitely on my Tom list.

Time to get a nap. I rest well on planes and with my headphones and eye mask in place I drift off to sleep.

48

Ahh, Milan. I love the hustle and bustle of this city, the food, the wines, and the language. Plus, I love the fashion. Jon knew I have always loved Italy. I don't look Italian with my Scandinavian heritage, my blond hair, and blue eyes. But, somehow my heart must have made a trip to Italy.

After landing and going through customs, I meet Lonzo, the man who is my driver, at the airport. Good thing he held up a sign with my name on it. He waits for me at my hotel, where I grab a quick shower and change my travel clothes. Now, I'm sitting in the stylish office of Mr. Luis Garcia drinking a cup of delicious Italian espresso. Looking out a window at the Duomo of Milan, I find an energy about this place. I'm ready to begin this leg of my new adventure.

Mr. Garcia greets me with a handshake and then a kiss on my cheek and apologizes for being a few minutes late as he tells me we will look at paperwork first and then have lunch. He instantly puts me at ease. Everything is in order, just like he explained on the phone and just like Mr. Jonse assured me it would be. Apparently, he and Mr. Jonse conversed after my meeting with him. It's good to know I now have two attorneys I can trust.

We look at all the documents together. Since Jon did everything and signed everything over to me, I don't really even have anything to sign. There is an account set up for taxes and fees that may come up. It's good for at least the next 10 years, he tells me. There is also an account for the salary of my driver, Lonzo, and for the groundskeeper. They are now my employees and I can either keep them or let them go. Jon only promised them that they would be guaranteed employment until I arrived. Then, it was up to me.

I look at Mr. Garcia. He tells me he thinks I will want to keep them, but not to make any hasty decisions. I nod.

The car is mine as well. And, the boat is available to me whenever I need it. All I have to do is have Maria call and the captain will have the boat ready. Wow.

Now . . . for the villa. There are 22 rooms, not counting Maria's suite. He tells me he employed a firm to inspect it before, during, and after all the renovations. Everything is up to date and up to code. A wireless network works throughout all the rooms, televisions are tastefully hidden but available, and the security system is state of the art. As for décor, that is up to me if I want to change anything. The basic furniture is in place, but there are still some finishing touches I will want to take care of once I get there. Maria can help me.

Surrounding lawns, gardens, and outdoor areas are all supervised and cared for by the groundskeeper. Maria works with him at the moment, telling him what to plant where. If I want to have anything changed, I just need to let her know.

Each of the four guest suites are on the second floor at the back of the villa. While not directly on the water, their private terraces do overlook Lake Garda.

Looking out onto the expansive gardens, the main part of the villa is on the ground floor, with a living room, a dining room, two small sitting rooms, and a stunning, fully furnished modern kitchen. Maria does some cooking, but will hire a chef anytime I want something special or when I want to entertain.

My suite is on the main floor as well. Apparently, there is a bedroom, a bath, a walk-in closet, a small sitting area, and an office, which also has a view of Lake Garda. He believes I will find it quite nice.

Pausing, Mr. Garcia looks at me and asks if Jon told me about his special, hidden rooms. When I tell him Jon made mention of them in one of his letters, he nods and informs me that Maria has been instructed to show them to me and that Tom will finish explaining them. He believes Jon gave one key to Maria, one to Tom, and was going to leave one for me somewhere. Pulling out my chain with the key on it that I found in Jon's case from his office, I ask him if this might be the one. He believes that it does look like it, but to ask Maria or Tom to make sure.

Still bewildered by all of this, I ask Mr. Garcia if there is anything I need to know about Maria. Smiling, he explains that she, Jon, and Tom had a working relationship. That really doesn't answer my questions about her and my husband, though.

Then I ask him if he knew what Jon did, other than engineering, that is. Telling me yes, as he was Jon's attorney here in Italy. He asks me to be patient for a couple more days.

Point blank, I ask him if Jon was a thief. Somewhat startled by my abrupt question, he asks me to wait until I talk to Maria and Tom before I form any opinions.

49

A fter looking at the rest of the paperwork, my curiosity is in high gear. I'm finally here, in Italy, and I want answers. I have been patient; it seems, for a long, long time. I remind myself that I will see my villa tomorrow morning, I meet with Tom possibly later in the afternoon, and I meet Jon's parents later in the week. Jon's sudden death seems like a lifetime ago. I'm still a little flustered, yet ready to find out more.

Now, sitting down for lunch at the Galleria Vittorio Emanuele, II, basically the world's oldest shopping mall, I relax with a glass of wine. Mr. Garcia asks if I would like a little background on how he and Jon met. Of course, I tell him.

Jon did some work for a client of his, who recommend Jon to him when he needed some help. Engineering, right? Sort of, he tells me. Jon knew about buildings, how they were constructed, how all the parts worked, and where to find all the doors and windows. Jon's knowledge and expertise were important when buildings needed to be inspected or accessed.

Still, not totally comprehending the scope of what Jon did, I nod and make a mental note to ask Mr. Garcia about Tom. Maybe that will help clear up some things.

Mr. Garcia went on to tell me that he and Jon became good friends when Jon was in Italy on a couple of assignments. Jon asked him to start looking for a villa but not to use his name when inquiring. In fact, Jon asked that the villa be put only in my name. Taxes would be paid through a corporation. When I asked why the secrecy, Mr. Garcia told me that was what Jon wanted.

Throughout the next several years, they had dozens of mutual clients. Jon and Tom were the ones Mr. Garcia recommended to particular people. What kind of people? He explained they were people who valued their privacy but needed Jon and Tom to accomplish a job for them. Confidentiality was a must.

Still not sure I comprehended everything Mr. Garcia told me, I decide it's best if I check out my villa and meet Maria and Tom. Maybe then I won't be so confused.

We finish eating, chatting, and drinking our wine and I head back to my hotel. Exhausted and exhilarated. I'm ready for bed.

At any rate, I'm in Italy. Tomorrow I will be at my very own villa. Time to toast Jon once more. And, get a good night's sleep.

I don't see the man on the street watching my hotel room.

50

⁜

It's early, I've checked out of my hotel, and I'm on my way to my villa. My driver, Lonzo, tells me to relax and enjoy the views. We'll be at our destination in a few hours, unless traffic delays us.

Maria will have lunch ready for me when we get there. Tom will meet us early this afternoon. My list of questions for Tom, as well as Maria, is growing every time I talk to someone else about Jon. It seems everyone knows one or two pieces about him but the one who knows it all is Tom.

I ask Lonzo what he knows about Jon and about Tom. He tells me Jon and Tom were the best in the world at what they do, or did. His brother, who lives in France, needed their services one time. If it weren't for Jon and Tom, his brother might have tried another method and could have even lost his life. What did they do for him? I wonder. When I ask Lonzo, he tells me Tom will have to fill me in on the details. He really doesn't know that much about it at all, except that Jon and Tom are fantastic. Great! I'm back to everyone being connected to Jon and I have no idea how.

Changing the subject, I ask Lonzo about my villa. He tells me he thinks it was owned by an elderly man who inherited it and couldn't afford to renovate it or keep it up. When Jon bought it, no one knew who the new owners were and what was going to happen to it. The grounds are beautiful and it sits on a spot on the lake with a fantastic view. He thinks I will like it. He tells me another brother and his nephew were the contractors for the renovations. They loved what Jon wanted done to the villa. He preserved the old look and charm but added modern amenities.

I ask what he knows about Jon's rooms that I keep hearing about. He has no idea what I'm talking about unless I mean the den. Probably not. He tells me to ask Maria as she could probably answer most questions about the villa for me. She lived there during the whole renovation. Plus, he tells me . . . there are a lot of rooms.

Lonzo explains that we are driving through the plains of the Veneto region of Italy and the soft hills of Bardolino, both famous for magnificent red wines. I am familiar with both regions, I tell him. He gives me the names of some places I need to visit. He knows the wine growers and they will treat me well, if I mention his name. I feel like I'm on my own private tour with my personal guide.

As much as I want to explore, I really want to find out about my villa and Jon's rooms first.

51

As we get closer, my normal curiosity about a new place I'm visiting is in full swing. I love traveling, seeing new places, finding out some unknown facts about a city and its history, and meeting new people. This is just like a new travel assignment, with a twist. A strange twist. Not at all like I'm used to when I travel someplace new. This one is personal.

As we wind our way along the south end of Lake Garda, Lonzo points out various landmarks. Ferries and fishing boats bob together on the impossibly blue water. The bright blue water does remind me of Lake Tahoe. But, unlike Tahoe, apparently the town of Lazise has medieval roots, with walls surrounding it and a dominating, yet picturesque castle, standing guard. This once fortified city still has ruins and walls remaining throughout. Lonzo explains that tourists love to visit the castle.

As we head north to the town I can see a small port, crowded with more fishing boats. Canals appear to be coming into parts of town and then emptying out at other spots. I ask Lonzo if those canals are similar to Venice. He tells me that Lazise is not built directly on pilings in the water as Venice is, but that the canals here are for the ferries and fishing boats to tie up closer to their destination. He continues on to tell me that canal transportation for tourists, locals, fishermen, and merchants is just as important here as in Venice. Many of the streets coming off various squares throughout the town end up at a canal. These then lead to the lake. Everything gets into and out of Lazise, via a canal off the lake, in one way or another.

He chuckles when I ask him if the canals are as confusing as some of them in Venice. He tells me there are good hiding places on the side streets of many of the canals. Just in case I would ever need to hide . . . I laugh with him.

Driving by, Lonzo points out the castle and its towers. I catch only a glimpse. Definitely, I will need to explore that. Various other towers and streets catch my eye as he tells me a little about the different places we are driving past. I'm in Heaven.

Off in the distance I see the Dolomites, part of the southern end of the Alps. Snow capped and more jagged than the Sierra in California, they appear to jut right out of the lake. Again, in some ways similar to Lake Tahoe.

Lonzo was right about the traffic he mentioned earlier. Surprisingly heavy, he tells me some days are like this. When I tell him I'm used to traffic in San Francisco, he just smiles and shakes his head.

Driving along the edge of town, Lonzo explains that my villa sits back from the lake. Apparently, I do have a private walkway to the water which includes my own small, sandy beach. Due to the snow melt, Lonzo tells me the water is cold year round. Probably not as cold as the Pacific Ocean, I think. He continues on to tell me that my driveway is gated and to enter I use an intercom system and a code. Hmm . . . no one ever mentioned that. When I ask him if he knows why so much security, he just shrugs and tells me Tom might know. Right. He probably will.

Sure enough, we pull up to a sturdy, wrought iron gate. Flanked by two stucco covered pillars, the wrought iron continues around the property in what I assume is a fence. We stop at a small box on one of the pillars, he announces his name, puts in a code, and the gate quietly slides open. Smiling, he looks back at me. It works. He tells me that Tom has my code, as each one of us has a different code. Lonzo thinks it's cool.

As the gate slides shut, Lonzo points out the beautiful gardens on both sides of the driveway. Shrubs, trees, flowers, fountains, and pathways are in perfect condition. It's obvious someone spends a lot of time keeping these looking impeccable. I can't wait to get out and explore these breathtaking grounds.

Lonzo then tells me to look at the front of my villa. It's perfect. I knew Jon wouldn't have anything ostentatious. It just wasn't his style, or mine, for that matter. Pulling up to the steps of the villa and stopping, Lonzo opens my door as a lady comes out of the front door. Beautiful is the first word that comes to mind. Continuing to look at her as she comes closer . . . stunning is more like it.

I'm terrible at guessing ages and once again all I notice is how stunning she is. One can't help but notice her flawless complexion, stylish hair, and absolutely well fitting outfit . . . no it's more of an ensemble. She's slim and only about five feet two inches tall. With a huge smile that lights up her entire face, she introduces herself as Maria and welcomes me in Italian and in English. She continues the greeting in Italian fashion with a kiss on both cheeks. Then a hug. She is so glad I am finally here. She tells me she is so sorry for my loss. With her hand to her heart, she tells me she misses Jon so much.

Directing Lonzo as he unloads my luggage from the trunk, she gives me another hug and tells me she has American coffee prepared for me. I'm still staring at her. She could be a model. Maybe she is. I have no idea what I pictured Maria to look like, but it wasn't this.

As I try to get my wits about me, a small Pomeranian dog and a large furry cat wander out the front door and sit on the steps. Maria apologizes and tells me she will keep her pets in her suite. Normally they only come out into the back garden area from her entrance, which is also at the back. Telling her I don't mind pets, they won't present any problems for me. Jon and I could never have any pets as we traveled often. Plus, the odd pair, small dog and a large cat, appears well mannered. She introduces the Pom as Chew and the cat as Mo. Chew licks me as I reach down to pet him, then does a little dance at my feet. Mo sniffs my hand and looks at me as if to let me know I'm just one more of his servants. Both apparently decide they like me.

Maria explains that recently, she has had some strange phone calls and one of the neighbors, who lives about three kilometers away, saw several people last week they didn't recognize. Even though there are plenty of tourists, this is still a small town where everyone knows everyone and their business. She's hoping her dog will at least make her aware someone they don't know is poking around. Apparently the Pomeranian only barks at strangers.

After all, when anybody sees someone new in the area, everybody knows about it. She tells me, everyone in town will know my name by this afternoon. That's just the way it is . . . everyone knows everyone, including their business.

Well, Jon, so much for keeping this quiet. Although, maybe that's not a bad thing. It certainly appears they all look out for each other. It's sort of like my neighborhood in San Francisco.

After giving both pets a command in Italian, they amble around the side of the villa and disappear. I think she told them it was time to eat . . . but I could be mistaken. I hardly had time to brush up on my Italian before I left the states.

Lonzo has disappeared with the first of my luggage and Maria asks if I want to freshen up before having coffee on the terrace. She tells me lunch will be ready after that or whenever I like. Then she tells me Tom has been slightly delayed but will be here in time for dinner. We can go over a meal schedule, etc. later. As we talk, or as Maria talks and I nod, she takes me to my suite.

I feel like a guest of this beautiful woman in her lovely villa.

52

Desperately wanting to ask to see Jon's secret rooms, I politely wait as Maria takes me directly to my suite at the back of the villa. I am on one wing of the back side as she points out her suite, which is across the courtyard in the opposite wing.

Opening the cherry wood door, my first glance tells me the whole suite is exactly what I would have picked out. Jon knew me so well. Obviously, better than I knew him. Maria can tell I'm pleased as I step inside to see it all.

We enter into a small sitting room, tastefully furnished in shades of pale blues and greens. A love seat faces the small fireplace. Book shelves, empty now, line two of the walls. There is only one picture hanging on the wall over the love seat. It's Jon. In San Francisco with the Golden Gate Bridge in the background. I took this one about two years ago and then couldn't find it on my camera or anywhere. I thought I deleted it by mistake and was so upset. I searched for a long time . . . it was the only recent photo I had of Jon. And, it disappeared. Now I know where it ended up.

Looking at Maria with tears of joy, shock, and surprise in my eyes, she tells me Jon knew I would cry when I saw it. She knows so much about my husband, it's kind of scary . . . but in a good way,

I think. All I want to do is stare at the photo, but Maria suggests we look at the rest of my suite.

Maria tells me that most of the decorating is finished and ready for me to move in. But, since Jon thought I would want to add my own touches, photos, and extras, I can change or add whatever I want. Sliding open a pocket door, we leave the sitting room and enter into a huge bedroom with another small fireplace along one wall. All three dressers, bed frame, dressing table, bench, and side chairs appear to be cherry wood. With pale tan walls setting off the richness of the wood, the affect is striking. A walk-in closet waits to be filled. I can do that! And, I will organize it just the way I want. Which means, not at all! I do see my luggage has all been brought in and neatly set by the closet. I'll deal with it right after my tour and our coffee on the terrace.

Maria wants to show me a special feature in my closet. A safe. Directing me to the middle of the closet is a table, which will be handy for packing and unpacking. On the near end of that table is a small door with a handle. Looking at Maria, I try to turn the handle, but nothing happens. In fact it doesn't turn at all. Maria smiles, goes to the other end of the table, and presses on the center of the panel. This is the end of the table you don't see when entering my closet. The panel slides open revealing a safe with a keypad on it. Ahh. Clever.

Telling me to pick the number I want as the code, she turns away while I set it. I then try to open it . . . and it works. Sweet. All the suites have safes in the same place. The alarm company said that was okay as long as we all had different codes to open them. She tells me that since the table cannot be removed, it would take an explosive to open the safe.

Right. This must be important.

To the right, is my bathroom . . . and what a bathroom it is. Telling Maria I could get lost in just this room, she laughs. She hopes everything I need is here. She tried to think of every possible thing I might want. And, she hopes I like the colors. Jon gave her an idea of what I like but she completed the color scheme and décor with towels, linens, art work, and amenities. When I tell her that these two shades of blue set against the white walls and fixtures is my favorite combination, she beams at me. She is even more beautiful when her smile lights up her entire face.

One window looks out over part of the lake. This whole bathroom is truly impressive. I may never want to leave this very spot.

Next, Maria tells me she wants to show me my office. Can it get any better than this?

It does. Once again, Jon thought of everything I might ever need. The soft yellow and white walls complement the dark cherry furniture. Book shelves, desk lamp, floor lamp, two printers, a laptop computer, comfy yet functional work chair, journals, pens, file cabinets, espresso machine, small sink and refrigerator, and an antique desk . . . which faces the most amazing view of Lake Garda. *Wow*, is all I can think. Off to the side, a French door leads to a private terrace, where my view is just as magnificent. This time I look right at the gardens. Again, wow.

Maria tells me to keep this door locked at night and especially when I'm not here. There is an alarm on this door, just like the rest in the villa. When I look at her questioningly, she tells me to lock this door and set its alarm. Pleasant, yet firm, in her suggestion.

This seems like a good time for me to ask about the rest of the villa. Telling me that we'll continue the tour as soon as we have coffee, we head out of my suite and back toward the main terrace.

I pinch myself. Am I really in my own villa?

53

Now, sitting on the terrace off the dining room, I'm looking at one of the many fountains in the garden. The sun warms me as I wait for Maria to bring the coffee. Somehow, I feel silly having her wait on me. I'm not used to servants and she certainly doesn't look like any servant I've ever seen. I'm curious about her. I wonder how she and Jon met. How long have they known each other? What does she see as her role now that I'm here and Jon is gone? Does she know Tom as well as everyone else seems to? Did she and Jon live here?

Opening one of the French doors, she comes out with a tray filled with delicious looking pastries and treats. I thought we were just having coffee, but just looking at the scones and flaky pastries makes my mouth water. As she pours coffee from a large French press, she tells me this is the only type of American coffee she knows how to make. Most of the time she uses the espresso machine in the kitchen.

When I tell Maria I like all types of coffee, she says next time she'll make espresso, or cappuccino, or Italian coffee, or whatever my heart desires. Once I tell her she doesn't have to wait on me, this seems like a good time to ask her some personal questions.

Before I have a chance, my cell phone rings. All I see is 'private number' listed on the screen. I don't know anyone who would be calling my cell phone that would be using a private number, so I decide to let it go to voice mail.

As the buttery pastry I'm eating melts in my mouth, I ask Maria if she baked them. No, she tells me, not with the wonderful bakery just a few kilometers away, actually on the edge of town. She gets all her bread and baked goods from them. She adds, with a twinkle in her eye, that they even deliver. If everything they make is this good and they deliver . . . I'm going to gain 300 pounds in a month. She doubts it, telling me I look as if I must work out. Never having a weight problem and always being active has worked for me until lately. Age must be catching up with my metabolism. I find myself needing to exercise more, especially if I'm traveling or spending time writing.

Her solution . . . just walk to the bakery. Not a bad idea.

I tell her I have many, many questions for her. To begin with, I want to know why Jon bought this villa. Then, I have questions about her and how she knew Jon. She nods and tells me she will start at the beginning. Great! Maybe I will now have a better understanding of many things.

Maria begins. First, she asks how well I know Jon's parents. They have told her they are coming here later in the week. When I tell her I have only talked to them once on the phone and can't wait to meet them, she nods. Let's start there, she says.

Before she can say anymore, my cell phone rings again. And, again it is a private number. Still not wanting to answer it, I let this one go to voice mail as well.

Maria refills my coffee and I help myself to yet another pastry. This cream filled one just begs to be eaten. Who needs lunch?

54

She starts . . .

Maria first met Peter and Diane when Sophie, her mother, was hired as their private chef. Sophie was a chef with her own restaurant in Paris, one Peter would frequent often. One night Peter and Sophie were talking. She told him she was getting ready to retire and he told her he was getting married to Diane in a week. Since both he and Diane had busy lives, he wanted to hire Sophie as their personal chef. Sophie's daughter, Maria, it seems, was just starting out as a model in Paris, so this seemed like a great move for Sophie.

Aha . . . I was right about her looks. She was a model.

Maria would visit her mother at Peter and Diane's villa in Austria whenever she could get away from Paris. However, she and Jon never crossed paths. For the next 10 years Sophie worked for Peter and Diane, although they treated her more like family than their personal chef. During this time, Maria's modeling career was changing due to the demand for taller, thinner models. Recognizing this, she decided to pursue her first love, interior design.

Another aha moment . . . no wonder the décor is so well put together in my villa.

While Maria's design career skyrocketed, she assisted with the art galleries Peter purchased, and when Sophie died in her sleep one night, Peter and Diane helped her adjust. Maria had never married and had no other family. Sophie was it. Peter and Diane became her family and she was immediately welcomed into their world.

Maria continued to assist clients with their décor and interior design all over the world, returning to Austria when she could.

One weekend she was back in Austria telling them of a particularly demanding client. He flew her to Dubai to redo his entire palatial condo, insisted that she have an affair with him, showered her with jewels, took her to expensive restaurants, and did not want to take 'no' for an answer. She finally had to lie to him and tell him she was engaged to a terribly jealous man in Germany. He apologized profusely and gave her a wedding present . . . a 10 carat sapphire necklace. When she told him she couldn't accept it, he told her to sell it and buy a house. After a few more days she completed his remodel and left Dubai...with the necklace. On her way to the airport she received a text from him that he would like to marry her if the man in Germany didn't work out!

Peter apparently didn't think this was as funny as Maria did, and told her he had a proposition for her. Their son, Jon, needed an assistant in Italy to work with some special clients all around the world. She would no longer have to worry about overly aggressive clients like the one in Dubai.

Maria didn't even know Peter and Diane had a son.

This was 15 years ago.

Even though I know better, she still looks like she's only in her forties. Her snow white hair is the only thing that might give her age away.

55

Pouring another cup of coffee and continuing on, Maria tells me she has worked for Jon and Tom on dozens of projects over the last 15 years. As I open my mouth to ask what kind of projects, she holds up her hand as if to tell me to wait. I shut my mouth and listen. She knows that Jon told me both he and Tom were engineers with extensive knowledge of buildings, how they were constructed, how they were laid out, and what materials were used. Sometimes they needed an interior designer to work with their clients. Now I think I'm starting to get the connection . . . until she continues.

Most of the time, those clients thought she was helping with design. In reality, she was canvassing the place for Jon and Tom.

What?

Telling me she will take me to one of Jon's rooms here in the villa and perhaps that will unravel some of the questions I have, she rises and motions me to follow her. Maria asks me if Jon gave me two keys. When I take out the white gold necklace with the key on it, she says that is the key to the first room she wants to show me. Tom can unlock the second room for me when he arrives.

We leave the terrace and walk into the villa, past the living room and den, and down a hallway I hadn't noticed before. The soft, pale beige carpet, here in the hallway, is the same as the rest of the house, the walls appear to be the same pale yellow, tasteful paintings decorate the halls, and the lighting is soft and understated. I'm beginning to think this hall leads to nowhere and that Maria may have taken a wrong turn. There's even a small table with a vase of freshly cut flowers on it, which looks to me like the end of the hallway.

Maria turns and smiles at me. I still can't get over how her face lights up when she smiles. She either realizes she made a wrong turn or there's more here than meets the eye.

Reaching under the center of the table she appears to grab something. Motioning for me to come and look, I bend over to see a small latch underneath the table. I look at her quizzically and she tells me to watch what she does.

As she pulls the latch towards her with one hand, she rotates the vase of flowers 90 degrees with her other hand. I hear a faint click and a panel along the right side of the hallway opens. Closing it the same way, she then tells me to try it. I manage to coordinate my right hand and left hand, pulling the latch and rotating the vase, and the panel opens like it did for Maria.

Wow . . . Jon apparently loved to design secret doors. I think I've opened several since his death.

Now, Maria states we will enter another short hallway. This is the first of Jon's secret rooms. I will need the key on my necklace to open the door to this one. The other room Jon kept secret is in a different wing of the villa. As we enter this hallway, the panel closes. She shows me a button that will reopen the panel for us to return to the main hallway. One single door is off to our left. This is the one that Jon's key opens. She asks me if I trusted Jon. When I say, absolutely . . . she smiles and tells me to keep that trust in mind as I enter this room. Maria will come in with me and try to explain what Jon was doing.

Opening the door, a light automatically illuminates a fairly large room. Shelves stacked several feet high, wooden crates that appear to be nailed shut, and several wall cabinets neatly fill about half of the room. A desk with a laptop and printer are off to my right. A small sink, refrigerator, sofa, and chairs are arranged inconspicuously along the far wall. The whole room is comfortable yet functional . . . as what?

Maria opens the doors on one of the larger wall cabinets. Stacked in protective clear wrappers are what I assume to be paintings. Did Jon collect art? Maria motions for me to look at them. Carefully inspecting one of the larger paintings, I notice the signature. I take a giant step back. A weak scream escapes my lips.

56

Gently, Maria takes my arm and moves me to the small sofa. Handing me a glass of water, she looks directly at me, reminding me to keep my trust in Jon. Nodding, I drink the water. Am I really here? Did I just see Picasso's signature on that painting? Time passes . . . I have no idea whether it was five minutes or five hours.

Gathering my wits about me, I fire questions at Maria. Is that an original Picasso? Is it genuine? Did Jon steal it? Was Jon an art forger or worse . . . an art thief? Why does he have these things here at the villa? Who does that Picasso belong to? Am I in trouble? Was Jon in trouble? What does Tom have to do with this? For that matter, what do you have to do with all of this? Are you a thief?

I'm positive I'm not making any sense to Maria. Still, she smiles and tells me she will continue on with Jon's story as soon as she shows me a few more items. In a drawer of one of the chests sits two familiar looking black jeweler's boxes. Wracking my brain, I tell her I've seen one exactly like this recently. It had the same jeweler's crest and everything.

As soon as Maria opens the first slim box, it hits me. This is the matching bracelet to the necklace Jon had in his safe deposit box . . . the necklace that had been stolen. The one which Joseph Barth's sister was wearing. That's why the boxes look so familiar. But, why is this piece here and the other piece in San Francisco?

Looking at Maria, I know what's in the other box . . . the magnificent emerald solitaire. Even though I was prepared for an amazing stone, when Maria opens its box, I am in shock. The size of the emerald is overwhelming. The deep green hue is breathtaking. I can only sit and stare at it. I need to tell her about the necklace in San Francisco; the one Jon had in his safe deposit box.

She realizes I have more questions but she tells me there is one other piece she wants me to see before we go back to the terrace. Then, she will tell me more about Jon.

Reaching into another chest, Maria takes out a small red box. Placing it on the table in front of the sofa where we are sitting, she carefully opens it. Inside sits a small golden statue. I don't recognize it. She tells me it is solid 24 karat gold and is worth approximately a million US dollars. It's at least 400 years old. Unbelievable! But, what the hell was Jon doing with this?

While I sit on the sofa and stare into space, Maria puts everything away, making sure it is all exactly in the right place. She then takes my arm and guides me through the doorway, out into the small hallway, and then back through the entrance by the table with the flowers.

Once back on the terrace in the late afternoon sun, I take a seat but can't even seem to think straight. My head is spinning, my brain is mush, and nothing seems to be functioning correctly.

Maria leaves me and then returns with another tray. This one has two wine glasses, a bottle of chilled Prosecco, and a plate with some small sandwiches. Pouring a glass for me, she offers a toast to Jon.

Now, she says, she will tell me the rest of the story.

57

I sit and listen. Telling me that Tom can fill in his part of the story better than she can, she attempts to give me a little history there as well. Maria starts by telling me that Tom and Jon first met each other in college and then went on to become engineers for the same firm in San Francisco. Tom only worked with Jon there for a few years; she isn't exactly sure how many.

When Tom's father was killed during a sting operation, the FBI looked appealing to him. He wanted revenge by catching the killers. She's not sure anyone ever found the ones responsible for his father's death. And, since Tom was an engineer, drug rings and sting operations weren't exactly his specialty.

Tom worked for a few years for the FBI, mostly helping track down big time thieves. On one particular art theft sting, the FBI was having trouble gaining access to a building where they assumed the thieves were storing the stolen art. There didn't seem to be any building plans anywhere.

Tom suggested that he and Jon might be able to piece together how the building looked, what it was constructed of, and how to gain access to it. Together they poured over plans they obtained from city workers and utility companies. And, sure enough, they figured it out.

It took a few months, but they gave the FBI what they needed . . . a way in. When the FBI recovered the stolen pieces of art, they offered Jon a job.

What? Jon worked for the FBI? When?

Well, Maria continued, Jon didn't exactly work for the FBI. He mostly consulted and used his engineering skills to assist them with building layouts.

Really? Why didn't he tell me about this?

No one except Tom, his boss, and Jon's parents knew anything about Jon's involvement with the FBI. Jon wanted it that way and it was safer . . . for everybody. These weren't nice people and they were stealing original art pieces.

I am so intent on listening to Maria while trying to piece together Jon's involvement in assisting the FBI, that my cell phone startles me when it rings. I practically jump out of the chair. I see the same 'private number' from earlier calls on the screen. Okay . . . okay, I'll answer it.

The voice on the other end is one I recognize. It's the Mexican policeman who talked to me when I found the dead body. He greets me and then gets right down to business. The medical examiner has completed the autopsy of the man I found on the beach. When the officer asks my husband's name, I'm confused and ask why he needs to know. He tells me it is important. Still not understanding what the dead man on the beach in Mexico has to do with Jon, I reluctantly tell him Jon's name.

The officer continues by telling me there is a connection between the dead man and my husband. The dead man had my husband's business card in an inside pocket of his jacket.

He also had my address in San Francisco and the address of the condo where I was staying in Mexico written on a piece of paper.

Then the officer informs me . . . the FBI is involved.

58

Maria can tell I'm upset as I give the Mexican policeman the address of my villa. He assures me I won't have to come to Mexico right away, possibly not at all. They already know that I didn't recognize the man. And, apparently they've checked out my story, when I arrived at the condo, what flight I was on, where I live in San Francisco, and the name of my attorney in the states.

Huh? I didn't remember giving them an attorney's name. But, they have Mr. Jonse listed as my attorney. I confirm he is and the policeman tells me to enjoy my visit in Italy.

Sure.

My hands are shaking as I put down my phone and pick up my glass of Prosecco. I feel like I should just drink from the bottle. Maybe that would help. Maria asks me to tell her what happened and I fill her in on everything . . . starting with how I found out Jon died, Mexico, my inheritance, Mr. Jonse, Jon's hidden room at our house, the extra passports, the two handguns, the hidden gold, and the jewelry Jon left for me in his luggage. Oh yeah, then I mention that I forgot about the weird and creepy experience at the bank owned by Joseph Barth, III.

Throughout my whole narrative, she nods quietly. However, when I mention Barth's name, Maria's eyes grow wide and she appears startled. She asks me to repeat what I just said about him. She asks me to describe in detail what went on at the bank that I thought was weird. Starting with the armed guards, Barth's advances toward me, and the visit Mr. Jonse and I made to the bank I then tell her about the necklace that matches the bracelet and ring here at the villa.

Definitely, she says I will need to tell Tom about the necklace and that experience at the bank.

Now she's the one with a wrinkled forehead. Hmm.

When I tell her I've felt like someone has been watching me, she asks when and where. Trying to remember, I fill her in as best as I can. Again, she says we need to tell Tom about this as well. It's probably nothing, but she knows we need to be careful at all times.

Looking at the clock, she says the chef will be arriving soon. Chef? She tells me she enjoys cooking but is not the chef her mother was, so for tonight we are having a dinner prepared by a local chef who owns a restaurant in town. It's a treat for all of us; Tom, me, and her. I tell her I need to unpack and want to take another look at my suite. No hurry, she tells me, as dinner will be ready about the time Tom gets here.

Checking out the rest of the first floor, I take a detour to my suite to wander through the living room, den, and sitting rooms. Now that I know Maria is a professional interior designer, it all makes sense. The whole place is classy yet comfortable. It's not stuffy or overdone. Colors are exactly the ones I would have chosen to go with the warm wood and to compliment the views. Windows seem to be placed to take advantage of all those magnificent views. I'll check out the guest suites later. I want to see the kitchen, but don't want to interrupt the chef. I can do that later as well.

And, I do wonder where Jon's other hidden room is and what could possibly be in there. More art?

Right now I need to unpack.

I'm still trying to wrap my brain around exactly what it was that Jon and Tom did. Did they do this full time? It must have paid well. This villa could not have been inexpensive and Jon left me all that money. What about engineering?

And, then what about the dead body in Mexico? Why would he have both Jon's business card and my addresses in his pocket? Does it really matter at this point? He's dead. I wonder who killed him. It certainly wasn't Jon. He was already dead.

I'm positive Jon did not have a heart attack.

59

Entering my suite, I feel my questions take a back seat in my brain as a soothing calmness comes over me. This is so relaxing and perfect for me. Those book shelves need to be filled. Jon knew how I loved to read. I'll ask Maria where I can find the best book stores in town. This would also be a good time to brush up on my Italian.

As I step through the doorway into my bedroom from the sitting room and head toward the closet to unpack, I notice my suitcases are on their sides, not neatly standing up like I remember. I know for certain they were standing up, just as if Lonzo carefully set them down. I must be more tired than I thought. On a closer inspection, I notice they are haphazardly placed and I don't think Lonzo would have just dumped them. He seemed much too particular about things than to just dump my suitcases in a pile.

Plus, I'm positive they were next to my closet doors. Picking them up and moving them into my closet, I take some time to put things away and hang up my clothes to get rid of wrinkles. I decide to change clothes before dinner. Reaching for the last suitcase, I notice the lock is broken. I use TSA approved locks but this one is damaged beyond repair. I think I would have noticed that going through

Customs. I wonder if Lonzo had something to do with that. This suitcase doesn't have anything special in it, either. Just more clothes, some of my journals, and a few pairs of shoes.

I'm wearing my new jewelry from Jon and everything of any importance is in my travel purse and carryon. Oh well, I can get a new lock.

As I turn to take my toiletries case into the bathroom, I notice the French doors to the terrace are wide open. I thought Maria closed and locked them when we left here earlier today. Apparently not, even though she told me to remember to do so. Since it's getting dark and cooler and since Maria was adamant about locking them, I will do that now.

With everything put away, a fresh change of clothes, and my suite safely locked up, I head back to the dining room. As I approach, I hear voices. I recognize Maria and I think I recognize the man from the airplane, which would be Tom. Finally. But, there seems to be another voice I don't recognize. Maybe it's the chef.

Rounding the corner, I see Maria waving her hands and talking very fast in Italian. Tom is there as well and he's just as involved in the conversation. The third voice belongs to a large man dressed in a uniform. Definitely not the chef.

As I enter through the dining room, silence replaces the talking. It's eerily quiet. All three turn and look at me. Did I forget to put on my clothes, is my hair standing straight up, or what?

Maria recovers first and introduces me as Jon's wife and the owner of the villa to the gentleman I don't know. He smiles, shakes my hand, and tells me he is sorry for my loss. He knew Jon and always liked him. She introduces him as the Chief of Police from town.

Apparently, there have been a few recent break-ins in the neighborhood. Nothing of any value has been taken, but alarms have been disarmed in order for the thieves to enter the other villas. He wants to know if we have seen anything out of the ordinary. I figure this would be good time to tell him about the doors in my suite and Maria confirms that she did indeed shut and lock them earlier today.

He tells us to be careful and to pay attention. Then he mentions that we need to have the alarm company reprogram our alarm system in the morning. Welcoming me again to Lazise, he apologizes that he had to meet me under these circumstances and reminds us to lock up.

As Maria shows the Police Chief out, Tom asks me how I'm doing. Making our way to the dining room, he says we have a lot to talk about.

No kidding, I think.

60

⬥⟡⬥

Again, Maria is the one who seems to have her act together. She has the table set and wine ready to pour as she disappears into the kitchen to inform the chef we are ready for our first course. Tom tells me he will answer all my questions but first he wants me to listen to him. What he tells me will most likely cause more questions, but if he can explain everything in chronological order it will probably help me make sense of many things.

Nodding, I agree. I tell him most of my earlier questions are written in my journal. But, it certainly seems I have more questions now, due to what has happened here at the villa. He smiles and agrees. Telling me to stop him anytime for clarification or a brief question, I assure him I will.

Maria and the chef enter with two platters of antipasto. Fat green olives, thinly sliced meats, a couple of small blocks of cheese, and a variety of small vegetables all fill one entire plate. Bread that smells like it just exited the oven sits on a board, surrounded by small bowls of bright green olive oil and dark, thick balsamic vinegar. All of a sudden I'm famished. Tom pours a crisp white wine as all three of us sit at one end of the dining room table.

Maria points out that the table expands to seat 20 comfortably.

When I want to have a dinner party, this table is wonderful.

Our chef introduces himself, briefly describes the remaining three courses for our dinner, tells us he is leaving, and that Maria has everything under control. I decide I need to pace myself for the rest of the meal if the other courses taste like the first one. Who needs more? The crisp wine compliments the salty meats and cheeses and doesn't over power the olive oil.

Tom waits until the chef has gone and then he toasts my arrival in Italy. He wishes it could have been under different, more pleasant circumstances. We all agree. As we eat and drink he starts talking.

Even though I already know, Tom tells me he and Jon met at Stanford. Both graduated in engineering, still hold several patents on building design components, and worked for a firm in San Francisco. I stop him and ask him why Jon never mentioned him to me. He explains that by the time I met Jon, he was already out of the picture as far as engineering goes.

Continuing, Tom tells me his father was killed about the time he and Jon were working on some major building projects together. His father was an undercover FBI agent tracking a huge ring of thieves, who were also into drug trafficking. Apparently, Tom's father had trusted the wrong person while undercover and that person turned him in. Tom was devastated.

Tom started asking the FBI when and how they were going to get his father's killer. They informed him that many times they were so close to catching the whole ring. But each time they came just a little closer, something would happen to stop them in their tracks. They had discovered a building complex that was being built in the Midwest. The problem was that no one had any drawings or plans for it. No permits were filed with any appropriate agency. Nothing. Tom suggested he work with the city as an engineer to see if he could get a copy of the plans. After much discussion and persuasion on the part of Tom, the FBI agreed. But, Tom had to take an 'assistant' with him . . . an FBI agent. The FBI wasn't about to send an untrained man into this arena.

Tom and his 'assistant', a geeky looking guy, posed as city inspectors and requested a tour of the building. They told the guard they needed a tour or they would have to red tag the whole complex.

Tom doesn't know if the guard was new or naïve, but he let them inside when no one else was around. That was all it took. The FBI swarmed the place, found stolen goods ranging from weapons to art to jewelry, plus a bunch of drugs worth millions on the street. In the end, they even found the weapon that had killed Tom's father.

Shortly after that, the FBI contacted Tom and offered him a proposition. They would send him to their training and he would specialize in areas where his engineering would be valuable. Tom could still work with Jon on some projects, but he would provide a service to the FBI as well.

Tom tells me that appealed to him, even though Jon tried to talk him out of it.

At first . . .

61

Tom continues with the story . . .

He worked for the FBI for a few years, with Jon helping him on different building designs. Jon never actually worked directly for the FBI. He was more of a consultant.

When one wealthy man from Florence, Italy, had some valuable art stolen and it surfaced in the US, the FBI became involved. Tom and Jon were instrumental in getting the artwork returned and the thief arrested. The Italian man contacted Tom and offered him and his partner a job. He knew of people that had valuable items stolen. Most of those items were never recovered. The Italian checked out Tom and Jon, he liked the way they worked, and he wanted to hire them. He didn't care if they still did engineering work on the side. But, when he needed them or someone he knew needed them . . . they were to work for him at a moment's notice.

They both agreed.

I told Tom I could understand how this interested Jon. He loved solving puzzles and these heists were just huge puzzles to him. Tom just smiled.

While I'm digesting all of this, Maria clears our plates and brings us our next course . . . pasta. Tom pours a Chianti wine and I inhale all the aromas drifting up from the delicate pasta, spicy sausage, rich tomato sauce, and block of Parmigiano-Reggiano. I will never have to eat again.

Tom continues to fill in the blanks . . .

Part of the arrangement in working for the Italian was for Tom to be the contact person, the one the clients met. Jon was to be the guy in the background, solving the puzzles. He was figuring out how the building was designed, where the stolen items were kept, how they would gain entrance without being noticed, and organizing what they needed to recover those items. No one ever met Jon. They would be in demand all over the world. The Italian had friends, relatives, and clients everywhere.

Throughout this part of the story Tom had not been referring to the Italian by name, so I ask what his name was and what he did.

Tom tells me they could only refer to him as the Italian. Until now. About a week ago he was killed in a boating accident in the Mediterranean. It's still under investigation. There's no way it was an accident, according to Tom.

Tom informs me his name was Angleo Fortini and he owned the largest shipping company in the world. He was worth billions. *Wow.* Also, he had some enemies. Some nasty enemies.

Are there any other kind? I think to myself.

There's more, Tom tells me.

Fortini's uncle owned this villa. When he was getting older and no longer wanted it, he gave it to Jon. Confused, I tell Tom that I thought Jon bought this villa. Tom explains he did buy it . . . for one Euro. That way it was a legal sale.

Tom looks at me and tells me . . . there's more.

Fortini's uncle had an affair with Maria's mother.

What?

Looking at Maria, she nods and smiles. She's often thought about getting a DNA test run to see if he was her father . . . but as of yet she's never done that.

62

Once again, Maria clears the table and brings our salad course. As if waking from a long nap, I shake my head and tell her I should be helping her. Nonsense. This meal is to welcome me she tells me. There will be plenty of times for me to help later.

Tom pours us another glass of wine and continues to talk.

I interrupt and bombard him with questions. How did Jon manage to work in all these trips? Why didn't I know what was going on? What exactly did you do? What does this have to do with the passports, money, and handguns I found in our home? And . . . ?

Stopping me in mid-sentence, he tells me he understands my questions. Asking me to let him continue, I nod.

Tom continues talking . . . He tells me that, at the beginning, much of Jon's work was completed at his office in San Francisco. Tom met with the clients, they then informed him what had been stolen from them, and he put them in touch with his contacts from the FBI or Interpol or Scotland Yard. Then, he and Jon would work out two things for their clients. One, they would figure out how to make the client's home or gallery more secure. And, two, they would offer their engineering expertise and assistance to the agency involved in getting the stolen goods returned.

That plan worked for many years. But in time, some thieves became more savvy and some clients more demanding. Tom and Jon found they had to adjust.

It was then that some paintings were stolen out of Peter's gallery in Paris. Jon became more involved and actually started some of the recovery work. In hindsight, this is probably what killed him. He was now a known partner in their recovery business.

Wait a minute . . . Why did the hospital tell me Jon had a heart attack? I don't get it.

Let's back up, Tom tells me. He'll get to that part soon.

Moving on . . .

Tom says they worked as a team from that point forward. Jon would arrange his work trips to coincide with my travel assignments or meetings he had to attend 'out of town'. Only out of town might mean Hanoi or Vienna.

Ahh . . . the passport stamps.

Most of the time they recovered art, jewels, or small artifacts thieves tried to sell on the black market. Most of the time they didn't even get involved with the thieves, other than to pose as buyers for something that was stolen. Federal agents from one country or another took care of arresting the thieves. Most of the time they never even had to fire a weapon. Most of the time . . .

Maria interrupts to clear the table and bring small slices of a layered dessert. If it tastes as delicious as it looks . . . Tom pours dessert wine and tells me he will explain the times it was dangerous.

Dangerous? How?

Telling me to take a bite and enjoy the delicious treat, he gazes at his glass of wine as if he's a thousand miles away.

63

We devour our scrumptious dessert and I wonder if I can lick the plate. Maria tells me she will give my compliments to the chef and Tom resumes talking.

They were in San Francisco. A necklace, missing for several decades, was spotted on a woman at a gala in the city. This was not an ordinary necklace. It had been stolen along with a bracelet and a ring, years ago, and the set was worth more than just money to the original owners. The whole story of how it was stolen once again surfaced, with rumors and speculations running wild.

I nod as Tom continues.

Tom did some investigating about the jewel heist and the woman seen wearing the stolen necklace. He found she was an ex-girlfriend of the hotel concierge in Paris where these jewels and many others had been stolen. None of them had ever been recovered. No one could ever make a tight enough connection for a conviction. Both the concierge and she disappeared shortly after the theft.

Again I nod, as Mr. Jonse told me part of this story. I'll tell Tom where the necklace is once he's finished . . . unless he already knows.

Tom also discovered the woman had a condo in an upscale building in San Francisco. Jon contacted the woman and told her he was the engineer in charge of renovations in her building. She didn't realize there were renovation plans so Jon arranged to meet with her at her condo to look over the plans to do so. She was most agreeable. Jon was going to take a look at her condo in depth, while taking notes and pretending to be measuring every spot. In reality, there were no actual plans.

When Jon arrived at her building the doorman let him in, as she had already informed the doorman she was expecting Jon. But, when Jon got off the elevator on her floor, her front door was wide open. Jon had been in this business long enough by now to know there was something not quite right. Calling her name, Jon entered, being careful not to touch anything.

No answer. Jon walked around the spacious condo, continuing to look everywhere. When he entered her bedroom, she was lying on the bed. Blood was everywhere. By now, Jon was alert to every sound. Glancing one more time at her, he noticed something bright clutched in her left hand, hidden from view unless the light from the window caught it just right.

Opening her hand with his handkerchief, the necklace fell out. Jon picked it up, stuffed it in his pocket, and decided to leave immediately. Using his handkerchief, he closed the door behind him and headed for the elevator.

Jon was going to alert the doorman that she didn't appear to be home. He wouldn't tell him he had gone inside. After all, the doorman did see Jon go up to her condo.

Once back downstairs though, the doorman had vanished. No one was in the lobby or anywhere to be seen. When Jon went outside, the door locked behind him. Jon could hear sirens in the distance, coming closer.

Instinct told him they were coming here. Who had called them? Where is the doorman? As the police cars rounded the corner, he opted to stay put. After all, most buildings have security cameras in their lobbies and he surely would have been observed entering.

Jon explained to the police that he was here to see a client and the now-missing doorman had let him in. But, he also told them his client did not answer her door. He assumed she must have forgotten her appointment with him. When he came back downstairs to ask the doorman to call his client, that doorman was nowhere to be seen. The police told him they received an anonymous tip that there had been a murder in this building. Jon said nothing.

When it was all said and done at the end of the night . . . there was no doorman and no security camera tape. Jon was not questioned again. Her death was ruled a suicide. Jon knew it wasn't.

And, Jon had recovered the necklace, which was now hidden in his coat pocket.

64

Maria suggests we head to the den to finish our wine while we listen to the rest of the story.

Once we get settled, Tom continues . . .

While Jon was recovering the necklace, Tom was researching the dead woman. He found out she was not really an ex-girlfriend. She was related to the concierge and was the sister of Joseph Barth, III, who owned a bank in San Francisco. Apparently, Barth did not want anyone to know of their relationship. His comment, when interviewed about her, was that they were estranged due to family issues and hadn't seen each other in years. Tom also discovered Barth had enough of his own troubles with the Feds. Plus, rumor had it he was nuts. Certifiably crazy, according to some.

When Tom told Jon about Barth, Jon remembered his name from the tennis club. He also remembered something being in the paper about an agency investigating his bank. But, that was about it.

Shortly after Jon recovered the necklace, Barth sought him out at the tennis club. Even though they didn't really know each other, Barth asked him several off the wall questions about jewelry. Jon side-stepped those questions by telling Barth he was an engineer who only understood jewelry when he bought it for his wife. Barth also asked questions about Jon's wife, which made Jon even more suspicious and cautious around him. He suggested dinner with Jon and his wife. Jon politely declined, saying they were busy. When Barth persisted and Jon declined, he had the impression Barth was upset about that.

Then, Barth suddenly switched gears and talked extensively about his bank. He insisted Jon use his bank whenever he needed to meet with a client. Barth told him about a private, wonderful meeting room he used to impress clients and guests. Security is state of the art so Jon wouldn't have to worry about anything. Jon thanked him and when he turned to leave, Barth reached for Jon's hand. He then gave him a card for a safe deposit box and told him he had some of the wealthiest people in the entire bay area as clients. According to Jon, the whole conversation was odd.

Tom and Jon informed the Banking Commission about this conversation . . . but not about the necklace. The Feds asked Jon to use the card Barth gave him to get a safe deposit box. They didn't really care what he put in it. They just wanted access to his bank through a person Barth wouldn't suspect.

For the next few months, Jon would go into the bank on one errand or another, record conversations, and take photos for all of the federal agencies investigating Barth's bank. Every time Jon visited, Barth would ask him questions that pertained to jewelry, specifically heirloom jewelry.

Both Tom and Jon knew that somehow Barth knew Jon had the necklace. They weren't sure if there were security cameras in his sister's condo or if the killer was still in the condo when Jon recovered the necklace. Now, Tom says they will never know.

When I ask why not, Tom tells me Joseph Barth, III was killed in an accident yesterday while fishing off Baja, California.

Whoa. My head is spinning. And, it has nothing to do with the wine.

Maria tells me I need to tell Tom what I told her. As he looks at me questioningly, I repeat my story once again.

When I finish, Tom says something is not right. He says he needs to think this through. Things don't seem to fit together for him.

He ponders out loud . . . why would Barth take me to the room in the basement? What was the purpose of doing that? Did he hope to get me alone? Maybe there are cameras in the room where Jon's safe deposit box was kept. Did Barth see me remove the case from Jon's box? He is glad I left the necklace with Mr. Jonse. It will be safe until Tom can return it to its original owner's granddaughter.

Changing our conversation away from Barth and the necklace, Tom reassures me that for years Jon wanted to let me know what he was doing. But, he felt it was too dangerous. In the last six months before Jon was killed, they had decided to take one last client and one last job. Then, they were retiring from this business. Both had more than enough money.

Okay, time for some questions.

I mention again the hospital told me Jon had a heart attack. What was the purpose of that? Tom looks at me intently for several moments. He asks if I can absorb what he's told me so far. I tell him I can and I think I have.

Then, he tells me there is more about Jon that I will find out this week. He asks if I'm ready to know it all. When I say yes, he asks me if I'm sure. I'm getting a little freaked out, but I know I can handle it.

Tom nods, looks me in the eye, and continues in a serious tone; more serious than I have heard him so far.

Jon was killed by Joseph Barth, III or an assassin hired by Barth.

When he asks if I remember the dead body on the beach in Mexico, I nod. Most likely, he tells me, that dead body was the one hired to kill me.

Plus, he could have been the one who killed Jon.

Maybe I can't handle it . . .

65

Then logic sets in. Wait a minute. Who killed the guy on the beach? Is that why he had my address in his pocket? Do the Mexican police know this? And, who has been following me? If that guy is dead, then it can't be him. Does Barth have more than one hired killer on staff? The more I think, the more confused I get.

Tom tells me to wait a few more minutes for him to finish the story. I ask for a refill of wine. I might as well get comfortable. Who knows if I will remember any of this in the morning?

Maria suggests we finish talking about Barth, the necklace, and Barth's bank.

When Jon decided to put the necklace in the safe deposit box, as a precaution he filmed the whole procedure. Tom was the only other person who knew the necklace was there. Jon kept the recording of that in the file in his secret room in our house.

Stopping him, I tell him I never found the key to that file cabinet. In one of Jon's letters he told me it was on his key ring . . . but I never found that, either. Tom seems a little concerned by this.

He tells me he has the second key to that file cabinet but he doesn't like not knowing where the other one is. He makes a note to check that.

Continuing . . . Jon was concerned about Barth and what he might do to get the necklace back. They were both still positive Barth knew Jon had it. Tom pulled some strings and the FBI, as well as the banking officials, both watched Barth more closely.

I ask Tom if he thinks Barth was following me and he tells me it's possible. It would be something he would do. Remembering his advances toward me and how overly friendly he was, I get the creeps just thinking about him watching me.

Tom tells me Barth was out of the picture for many years, until lately. He's not sure why everything surfaced with the necklace. Barth had to know his bank was in trouble. Maybe he wanted the necklace in order to get the reward so he could leave the country. Maybe his hired thugs were threatening him. Who knows?

Tom is sure the FBI and Banking Commission will be conducting a full blown investigation now that Barth is dead. Tom makes another mental note to himself to make a phone call to the FBI.

Taking a drink of wine, Tom tells me Jon was like a brother to him.

Throughout the next several years they worked for clients referred to them by Mr. Fortini. Some came to them by word of mouth. Their clients wanted no publicity. Tom and Jon recovered uncut jewels, jewelry, art, paintings, sculptures, artifacts, weapons, and money. Everything was discreet. Their clients paid them well. And, most of the time, things were accomplished within the law. FBI, Scotland Yard, Interpol, and other agencies were often involved or at least informed . . . many times after the job was completed. Often, thieves were caught and then prosecuted.

Jon and Tom had a special bond with one another. They complimented each other so well. Tom really wishes he could have met me when Jon was still alive.

It's late. Maria and Tom both have more, much more, to tell me about Jon. But, Maria tells me that we will continue this over breakfast in the morning. For now, we all need to get a good night's rest.

As if I could rest. My mind is in overdrive as I head back to my suite.

Checking the doors and locks, everything seems to be in order.

Except . . . my closet doors are wide open. I know I shut them. I might not be neat and organized inside my closet. But, I always keep my doors closed so no one can see inside.

Turning on another light in my closet and looking around, everything in here seems to be just like I left it as well. Maybe I was in a hurry and didn't close the doors all the way. I begin to inspect my suite more closely.

Wait . . . my travel purse is not where I left it. In fact, I don't' seem to see it at all. Hurrying out of my suite, I run full force into Tom. Grabbing me, frantically he asks what is wrong. When I tell him my purse is missing, he says his suite was tossed. I'm about to ask him what he means when Maria comes running down the hallway. Her dog and cat apparently have been drugged.

We call the police . . .

66

Two hours later, the police have taken our statements, inspected the villa and grounds, taken photos, and left. Nothing seems to be missing. My purse was found out on the terrace, as if someone had hastily dropped it there. Since I had removed anything of value and placed it in my safe, the purse was just laying there with the remaining contents scattered around it. Tom had several drawers emptied onto the bed but again, nothing was missing. Maria's Pomeranian and cat are waking up. They most likely will be fine. Her suite was not ransacked at all.

Maria suggests we try to get some sleep and go over everything at breakfast. Once again, we all head to our suites. By this time, I can hardly keep my eyes open and I literally fall into bed. Figuring I will probably have nightmares, I'm surprised when I wake up seven hours later and feel refreshed.

Is that coffee I smell?

After a long, hot shower I head to the breakfast room. Maria and Tom are already there with coffee and more of those delicious pastries. Helping myself, I ask if either of them managed to get any sleep. Both of them look at me as Tom tells me to sit down.

What?

Tom starts . . . the police from San Francisco called. There was an attempted break in at my home there. The alarm was partially disabled and the thieves thought they could break in undetected. What they didn't realize was that I have two alarms and the silent one alerted the police, who just happened to be close by. They caught two of the thieves red-handed. One more may have escaped. They aren't sure and the thieves aren't talking. When they sent the photos to Tom this morning, he told them he recognized one of the men. He was Fortini's private assistant. Maria confirmed it, saying she had had Mr. Fortini and his assistant here at the villa for dinner with Jon.

Tom is disturbed by all of this. I can tell by just looking at him. Tom shakes his head and tells us he had trusted Fortini's assistant for years. He wonders how long he was living a double life.

Me . . . I'm disturbed about the attempted break in at my home.

What is going on?

Tom says he needs to make a couple of phone calls and that we will resume our talk about Jon at lunch. The alarm company is coming this morning to reprogram our alarm system. He asks Maria if she has shown me where the safe is in my suite. We both nod. I tell Tom that I'm glad I used it yesterday. Also, after lunch we will take a look at Jon's other room here at the villa. In the meantime, he tells me that I can explore the guest suites and the grounds.

Tom leaves Maria and me to finish our breakfast. My cell phone rings. It's Mr. Jonse's private line. He asks if everything is okay. When I tell him we've had a few mishaps here but Tom is handling them and when I reassure him I'm fine, he seems relieved. Apparently, he had a message on his private phone that I was involved in an accident here in Italy. The caller was difficult to understand and he couldn't trace where the call originated. He tells me to let Tom know. He's quite disturbed by the call. I make a note to tell Tom.

67

Telling Maria about the call, she agrees we need to let Tom know as soon as we see him. Then, I ask how Chew and Mo are feeling this morning. She tells me her pets are just fine but still a little dopey. She was so glad nothing happened to them. She doesn't understand how someone was able to drug her cat. He doesn't take food from anybody like the dog does! She figures the thief must have given Mo an injection. And, that makes her mad.

Asking if I would like to join her, she tells me she is ready to let them outside for a little while. We make our way to Maria's suite and then to the gardens. Wandering around, she points out various plants, flowers, and shrubs. She designed all of the gardens with the help of a landscape architect. She loves the way the paths intersect with fountains and benches. Her smile lights up her face when I tell her she did an amazing job. Chew, the Pomeranian, yips and runs around our feet as we walk. Mo, the cat, ambles off in search of sunshine or a bird. They both seem to have recovered nicely from the drugs and everything that happened last night.

Maria asks me if I'm concerned. When I ask her about what, she says all of this . . . Jon, his secret life, his death, the attempted break in at my home in San Francisco, the break in here, all of it. Truthfully,

I tell her my life was normal before Jon died. Or, at least I thought it was normal.

Now, my husband has been killed, I find out he led a very secret life for over 30 years, I discover a secret room in our home, I inherit an amazing Italian villa, and I'm about to meet his parents for the first time. In addition, on a beach I find a dead body who could be the one who killed my husband, I appear to be at the center of several break-ins, and I'm beginning to believe I may be crazy. Concerned? Not at all. Confused? You bet I am.

She chuckles and tells me she can fill me in on a few pieces Tom left out. Until recently, what Jon and Tom did was rarely dangerous. In fact, she helped them with several clients. She could gain access where two guys could not. People loved to talk to her about interior design and decorating; even thieves. And, some of these thieves were not the stereotypical thugs. They were wealthy, upscale people just like the ones they were stealing from. When I tell her that confuses me, she continues.

Some people like to have it all, especially if they know someone has a better, newer, more expensive piece of art or jewelry than they do. They just want what the other guy has. Then there are those that want to steal whatever it is and sell it to the highest bidder. They're in it for the thrill. The one thing they have in common is their egos. Some will brag about what they've done, others will say they knew who stole a certain piece, and yet others will boast that their art can't be stolen. Whose ego is bigger?

Often, those egos will talk to an unassuming interior designer. Especially when she strokes those egos and tells them they need a magnificent room to display their fabulous collection! She tells me I would be amazed to learn who has stolen what and what her clients have told her.

When I ask if she's afraid for her life or afraid someone will recognize her, she smiles. That's where Jon's second room here at the villa comes up in our conversation. We'll go there after lunch.

Calling her pets, she wants to show me something else in my suite. Something Jon had installed in case I needed to hide.

What?

68

With Chew and Mo safely back in her suite, Maria and I go to mine. She guides me to the bathroom.

Every time I walk in here, I am amazed at the size of this bathroom. Just as impressive is the size of the walk-in linen closet in the far corner. Thinking to myself and chuckling . . . I could hide a small family here if I needed to. Just then, Maria again tells me that if I ever need to hide . . . this is where I should come.

Hide?

Maria directs me to the linen closet and opens its door. She walks right in, reaches behind the stack of fluffy white towels on the right, and touches a keypad. What's a keypad doing in my linen closet, I wonder?

Maria explains that it has both her fingerprint and mine memorized and will open a small door that leads to a tunnel.

What the hell? Hide? Tunnel? Did Jon think of this or was it already here?

Maria tells me the tunnel feature was already here and Jon just improved upon its design. Apparently Fortini's uncle, who was the original owner, was a little paranoid. Since he had many friends in questionable businesses, maybe he was justly paranoid. Anyway, he just had the escape route. Jon added the keypad feature.

Questioning Maria, I ask where it goes. Let's try it, she suggests and tells me to touch the keypad behind the towels. When we step in and I touch the keypad, the door to the linen closet shuts and another door opens to our right. She tells me that once this happens, the door to the linen closet will be locked from the inside. No one in my bathroom will be able to open the linen closet door without breaking it down.

We enter the doorway into the tunnel and a soft light illuminates a pathway. Looking at Maria, she motions me to follow the path. The walls and floor are brick with lights along the way to guide us. I have no idea how far we walk, but we turn a gentle corner and we come to a couple of steps and a door with another keypad on it. I press on the keypad. The door opens as we exit the tunnel and enter the garden by the largest fountain. Huh. I didn't even see this doorway from the garden when we were here this morning.

Confused, I look at Maria. She instructs me to step into the garden as the door quietly shuts behind us. Situated between the trees on the edge of the garden, it doesn't even really look like a door. You could find it, but you certainly don't notice it right away. Asking her how we get back, she says to do exactly what we did to get here. Only this time, the keypad for my finger is at the base of one of the trees. Disguised to look like a normal garden stone, I turn it over and sure enough . . . a keypad.

Pressing my finger on it opens the door in the trees and we disappear back into the tunnel. Pressing the keypad in the linen closet, the door opens to the bathroom and we are back where we started. Sweet . . . I feel like James Bond.

It's just about lunch time, and since Tom should be finished with his calls, we head back to the terrace off the kitchen. Our chef from last night left us an amazing lunch in the refrigerator and I help Maria get it ready for the three of us.

Tom gets there about the same time we have everything ready and tells us he has more information on several of our latest issues. I tell him about the call from Mr. Jonse, where I supposedly was involved in an accident, and he says that's one thing he wants to talk about.

It seems my driver, Lonzo, was killed early this morning in a strange accident while driving on a winding road north of here . . . in the car Jon left here for me.

69

All of us sit and reflect while we digest this latest tragedy. I'm dumbfounded. What the hell is going on? Tom tells me he has made some more phone calls which may stop all this madness. In the meantime, he needs to finish telling me about Jon.

I ask if we need to check out Jon's room here and the one back in San Francisco at my home. I also ask Tom what needs to be done about all the passports, money, gold, and handguns I found.

He tells me everything all fits together and I will see the big picture once I hear what he has to say. Then we will go to Jon's other room here.

Tom starts by telling me that Jon kept the recovered stolen items here in the room Maria already showed me. It was a safe place to keep them until they could be returned to their rightful owners. The items that are in the room now were all part of a major heist in Vienna about a year ago. An international banker had them stolen from his villa while he was in Geneva on business. He had just had a new alarm system installed and couldn't figure out why it didn't work like it was supposed to.

Jon was the one that discovered the company installing the alarm was a front for a group of thieves. Tom was just informed by Interpol that the thieves have been apprehended and are awaiting their sentencing. The one who hired them was none other than Joseph Barth, III. One of the thieves suggested that Interpol look at Barth's private vault in the bank in San Francisco where they say he kept other stolen items.

No one, including Interpol, Tom, or the thieves, believes Barth accidentally died while fishing, either.

The items here are going to be picked up by a courier for the banker from Vienna. Wow! Talk about strange tales.

Tom continues on to tell me both he and Jon took extra precautions in just about everything they did. That's why he is so confused by the man or men following me. There should have been nothing to connect me to Tom or Jon. In the meantime, he's still working on who has been following me and how they seem to know my every move.

As for the break-ins here, the police feel they are local thieves. Several villas have been hit lately and only electronics have been taken. I can tell he's not convinced. However, that doesn't explain the attempted break-in at my home in San Francisco.

The Mexican police called Tom and have turned the body I found on the beach over to the FBI, as they are convinced he was the one who shot Jon. When I ask how that man died and wound up on the beach, Tom takes a drink of wine and stares at me for a moment. Then he asks if I remember him on the plane from Mexico to San Francisco. When I tell him yes, he asks if I wondered what he was doing in Mexico.

Since I really never thought about it at the time, I look at him and ask him what he was doing in Mexico. He tells me he was there to make sure I was safe. He had found out I was this man's next target and Tom was not going to let me get killed. He owed that much to Jon. How did he know that? Tom was tipped off by a trusted FBI informant and it turns out the informant was correct. The man was there to kill me.

Why?

Tom tells me he's positive the man was hired by Barth, who wanted revenge on Jon. Killing Jon wasn't enough. No one will ever know the real reason why Jon was murdered.

At any rate, Tom followed that man one night as he came toward Marissa's condo where I was staying. The man was hiding in the shadows as I finished my dinner and was getting ready for my walk on the beach the night before I found him. When he went back to his hotel, Tom followed him.

The next morning when the man went to breakfast, Tom entered his room. That's when Tom knew for certain he was going to kill me. He had my routine written down, photos of my walks and where I sat on the beach, every angle into my windows mapped out, and everything ready to apparently shoot me from a distance.

Early that evening, while I was ordering my last dinner, the man approached my window. Tom crept up behind him and strangled him. He decided to just leave him on the beach and partially cover him with sand to make him look like a drunk who had fallen asleep. While Tom was covering him up, a couple taking a walk on the beach asked if Tom needed any help. He thanked them and said he was helping his friend. He did not have time to completely search his pockets. After the couple moved on, Tom piled some more sand around him and figured the beach crew would find him the next morning.

Instead, I tripped over him!

He was surprised when the Mexican authorities told him the man had my address and Jon's business card on him.

70

Tom is convinced the series of accidents surrounding people that are somehow connected to Jon are related. Even though Jon has been dead for a while, these incidents keep getting closer to me. I seem to have had some form of contact with most of the people that have died recently, and that bothers Tom. His FBI training and his instincts tell him these are not just coincidences.

It's almost as if someone thinks I know something. Plus, Tom has a call in to find out more about Lonzo. He remembers that he and Jon had done some business with one of his relatives in France, but he didn't really know Lonzo. Tom is wondering if he could have anything to do with the break-ins here at our villa and the neighboring ones, too.

I tell Tom that Lonzo told me he thought highly of both he and Jon.

Also, Tom says he's confused why Mr. Jonse would receive a call about me being in an accident. Did someone assume I was going to be in the car with Lonzo?

Enough speculating. Tom wants to fill me in some more. But, first he wants me to start at the beginning and tell him what I did after Jon was killed.

I go through the whole scenario from the police coming to my door, the hospital morgue where I could only see Jon for a few minutes, the strangers I felt have been watching me, finding Jon's extra passports, gold, and handgun in my closet, going to Mexico, finding the dead body, and then full circle to the contents of Jon's manila envelope.

Then, Tom asks me what was in the envelope and to tell him about everything I found in our home. I tell him about Jon's letters detailing people, about the papers with what appears to be Jon's codes for clients and jobs, and about the hidden room with the file cabinet that I have yet to find the key, about the second handgun, and the deed to this villa.

All the while, Tom's nodding. Okay, he'll give me what few explanations he has.

First, the sheet with codes and numbers. It is indeed Jon's way of keeping track of the clients and what we did for them. Jon was correct in telling me to destroy it. I tell him I made two copies, both which are hidden in my home and the original that is here in my travel purse. He says he'll look at it later and then destroy it.

As for Jon's hidden office, in the beginning it was just a precaution. For a while he did keep some things there. He didn't want to keep anything in his engineering office that wasn't strictly engineering. Jon's file cabinet had the video recording of Jon placing the emerald necklace in the safe deposit box at Barth's bank. That recording can stay there for now.

As for Jon's notes on people, we can destroy those as well.

Now, Tom wants to explain about the extra passports, handgun, gold, and money. There were times when Jon or he had to travel under assumed names. They needed official documents proving who they were and money that was 'clean'. That handgun was not registered to anyone and again was a precaution. Tom's handgun is registered.

I ask about the other one I found. Tom believes Jon wanted me to learn how to shoot and that he was going to teach me but he died before that happened. Would I feel better about strangers following me? Maybe.

I ask about the gold. Is it really gold?

Yes, Tom tells me it is. They had recovered it fairly recently when they were looking for a painting that had been stolen from a gallery in London. The gallery was owned by Jon's father, Peter. Peter believed a supposed art dealer had pulled a switch on the manager at the gallery and sold him a forgery, while stealing an original by another artist. It turns out several different galleries were looking for the same man for the exact same reason. Tom, posing as a big time art buyer, arranged a meeting with this supposed art dealer. Two days before that meeting, Scotland Yard contacted Tom to let him know the art dealer may have also been involved in stealing several small gold bars from a prince in Egypt. They wanted Tom and Jon to be on the lookout for those as well.

Jon was to disarm the alarm system and enter through a maintenance area while Tom was meeting with the dealer in a salon off the main gallery. It all went perfectly, except Jon never found the painting that was stolen from his father's gallery. He found plenty of other stolen art and the gold bars, though. Removing everything took a little longer than they had hoped but it all worked out. Except, for not recovering the painting from Peter's gallery.

When Tom and Jon returned the gold bars to the prince, he insisted they keep some as a reward. They tried not to accept the gold, but he wouldn't have it any other way. This was about four months before Jon was killed.

71

Maria interrupts us to ask if I would like to make a trip into town with her. She wants to show me some sights and pick up some things at the street market. Plus, that will give me time to digest what I've learned from Tom and give Tom some more time to finish his phone calls.

Peter and Diane will be here tomorrow, so she needs to stock up on some food. She's going to attempt to make some of their favorite dishes that her mother used to make for them. She tells me I can help. Not sure if that's the way I want them to finally meet me . . . I agree anyway. I grab my camera.

Normally, Lonzo would have been available to drive us into town. We both still shake our heads at that. And, now that I think about it . . . why was he driving my car? Didn't he have his own car? Maria is just as puzzled as I am. She says he never drove the car Jon left for me. Never.

No point in us dwelling on that right now. I guess the authorities will have to sort out that mess and why my car was involved. We take Maria's car and head into the street market, in the center of town. Maria points out landmarks on our way . . . the Castle, San Zeno Church, S. Nicolo Church, the Venetian Customs House, and more of the canals and olive groves. Parking on a side street, we make our way to the market. Vendors come here daily to sell their goods. Locals wander from one stall to the next, filling their bags as they walk and talk. Everyone is smiling, talking with their hands, and laughing. It's as much a social event as anything.

Maria tells me some of the items she needs and hands me a bag and some Euros. I follow her for a while, meandering around all the stalls, greeting the vendors, and snapping photos. Samples of meats, olives, olive oils, wines, and breads are offered. I stop and smell some of the spices and take some more photos. There's a dog waiting patiently for a handout from one the butchers. When handed a small bone, he takes it gently. I could have sworn the dog smiled at the butcher. I capture that look in a photo. Great shot, I think to myself.

As I turn to look at some handmade soap, I catch a glimpse of a man who appears to be looking at me. I believe I've seen him somewhere but I can't quite see his face. It's more of a shadow. As I peer around another couple looking at the soaps, he's no longer there. He couldn't have just vanished into thin air. Am I paranoid because of all the things that have happened lately? I tell myself to keep an eye out for him again. I'll look for Maria and alert her as well.

Not seeing Maria immediately, I wander down another aisle to sample some cheese and a few different olives. With numerous shades of greens and purples, arranged by size in their own bins, these olives just beg for a photo. They glisten in the sunlight. Definitely good enough to eat. Finding a couple things Maria told me to buy, I add those to my bag.

When I see a lady selling table linens, I stop and find one that reminds me of our lemon tree in San Francisco. We have a brief conversation in Italian and English about her linens. When I pick up the one with bright yellow lemons on it and ask the price, a man bumps into me from the right side. Saying 'excuse me' in Italian, I step aside as he tries to brush up against me again. He attempts to grab my small handbag off my shoulder, but the lady selling the linens is quick. She slaps his hand as he grabs my arm and he quickly disappears into the crowd. In half Italian and half English, she tells me they have had a problem with certain gypsies trying to steal handbags and purses. I'm still paranoid.

Maria arrives just as I'm paying, tells me she has everything she was looking for, and asks if I'm ready to leave. When the lady tells her about the gypsy trying to steal my handbag, Maria says we need to tell Tom. Asking both of us if we can describe him, we tell Maria it happened so fast neither of us can be sure what he looked like.

As we make our way back to Maria's car, a man materialized out of a doorway several feet away and walked in the other direction. Looking at each other, we ask ourselves if we just imagined he was waiting for us or if he was shopping at the market the same as we were. He did have a bag with him.

We're not sure.

72

Back at the villa, Maria and I recount our story about the man in the doorway. I also tell Tom that I thought someone was watching me at the market and about the gypsy trying to steal my handbag. He's concerned about all of it. Especially after his phone calls this morning.

Unknowingly, Tom and Jon stepped into quite the mess, starting with the jewelry from the countess in Paris. Tom made and received several calls over the last couple of hours and found out Barth had quite the elaborate, yet nasty, plan worked out. It all revolved around Jon and his family.

Tom also learned Barth had quite the host of hired guns in his employ. If his hired thugs couldn't get their job finished, Barth would have them killed. Nice guy.

Apparently, their main mission was to confront Jon, find out what he knew about the missing jewelry, recover it, kill him, and then kill me. Somehow Barth knew the necklace was in his own bank. He figured Jon knew where the rest of the pieces were and wanted his hands on those as well. That's why he had Jon killed.

He sent one guy to threaten me in Mexico. Then, he was supposed to kill me. But, that didn't work out so well. When he discovered that man was dead, Barth was infuriated.

Apparently, before I went to Mexico, the plan was for me to meet with Mr. Fleetwood, who I thought was our attorney. In reality, he was one of Barth's men. Fleetwood was supposed to find out from me what I knew and what I had recovered from Jon's things and will. Instead, for some reason, Fleetwood fled to Italy and the meeting with me never happened. Barth found out where he was and had Fleetwood killed.

Yikes. It's getting worse.

Lonzo was really an innocent victim in Barth's sick game. Lonzo was approached a couple of days ago and given a huge sum of money to take me for a drive around the lake once I arrived here. He was to tell me Jon had some special places he wanted me to see. At first he thought it was strange, but the guy that hired him mentioned Jon several times so he figured it was okay. Plus, he was to use my car. When he told his wife about this, she was uneasy.

It turns out Lonzo decided to make a trial run to make sure the car was working properly before he came to offer me a ride. He called his wife from a village on the lake to tell her he was coming home. He didn't really see any of the places the guy mentioned and he wasn't sure I would want to take a ride just to take a ride. That was the last his wife heard from him. The police told her he must have fallen asleep at the wheel and hit a tree at a high rate of speed. She didn't believe it for a minute.

Tom agrees with Lonzo's wife. He suspects the brake line was cut or something else was tampered with on the car.

It seems the man who gave the money to Lonzo, was shot to death shortly after that. Apparently, somehow, someone knew I wasn't with Lonzo.

Oh my goodness . . .

Next, Tom learned Barth had men lined up to steal more of Peter's paintings from various galleries around the world. He was going to keep them in his secret vault room at his bank. He had been accumulating other paintings over the last decade.

I am so glad I didn't take more time in that room. I might have discovered something I shouldn't have. And, no wonder the guards were armed and overly cautious.

Finally, Tom tells us . . . it was discovered Barth was going after Jon's parents.

The good news in all of that is the art thieves were apprehended in Florence. As soon as one of the thieves started talking, they all couldn't talk fast enough.

73

From those thieves, the authorities discovered enough to put Barth away forever . . . if he wasn't already dead. A whole complicated tale of thievery and deception unfolded. As suspected, Tom learned the ring leader was Joseph Barth, III, who had hired contacts in many places around the world. According to one of these thieves, Barth was truly crazy. Probably psycho. They were all afraid of him. If he didn't like what you did or didn't do, he'd kill you himself.

The thieves mentioned one of the other men as Fortini's untrustworthy assistant. Apparently, he was one of the men who, just recently, tried to break into my home in San Francisco. In a side note to that, Tom found out he hanged himself in jail early this morning. When the two men who were with him in San Francisco found that out, they began to spill everything. The FBI, Scotland Yard, and Interpol have enough information to convict a whole group of people in the States and in Europe.

Whew!

Whoever said the life of a travel writer was boring?

Now, Tom is finally convinced everyone connected to Barth is either dead or in jail. Several attempts at stealing art from Peter and others have been thwarted. Unless there are more reports of attempted break-ins at my home in San Francisco, I should be safe there. Plus, there don't seem to be any more viable threats on my life.

But, Tom is still very concerned about several things.

Specifically, the man I keep seeing, the attempted break-in here at the villa with Maria's pets being drugged, and getting the paintings and artifacts returned to their rightful owners. The gypsy doesn't really bother him . . . he probably is just a gypsy looking for an easy purse to grab.

Now, he tells me it's time to show me Jon's other hidden room here at the villa. With all this confusion I had forgotten about it. Maria agrees. She reminds Tom that Peter and Diane will be here tomorrow, so it would be best if everything is explained to me by then. She tells Tom I need to know the rest of the story before their arrival.

Tom asks her if she showed me the escape route in the linen closet in my bathroom. Telling him we already checked it out, Tom nods absentmindedly, like he's deep in thought. Maria asks if he's okay. He nods again and then tells her there is something bothering him. She agrees. She's had a feeling about something ever since I arrived and started telling her what has been happening to me.

They both stare into space as if I'm not there. Not wanting to break their silence and their thoughts, I sit and try to remember if there is anything else I haven't told them. Finally, Tom looks at Maria and says he has an idea. An idea he should have thought of before . . .

Tom asks if I will get my travel purse and the sheets of names and numbers Jon left for me. He tells me it's important to bring both. Thinking he obviously has a plan, I head to my suite to grab my travel purse out of the closet.

When I return from my suite, Maria and Tom are deep in conversation. They look at me like I have grown two heads as I enter the sitting room.

What . . . I ask them.

Tom responds first and says they have some questions for me.

He begins by asking when I first remembered seeing a man following me. Was it before or after Jon died? Do I recall how many times? Did I ever get a good look at him? Do I think it was the same man? Specifically, did he have the same build and wear similar clothes?

Second, when do I remember strange things happening? What exactly happened at the hospital morgue, the funeral service, and the burial? Was there even a burial? If so, did I go to the burial?

Third, do I always carry this travel purse? Specifically, did I have it when I went to Mexico, Mr. Jonse's office, and to Barth's bank?

Fourth, has my home been broken into before or after Jon died? How did I receive the manila envelope from Jon? What else can I tell them about the things from Jon's office?

Last, where is my cell phone? Am I the only one to use it?

Whoa . . .

74

Taking a deep breath, I try to answer as many of the questions as I can for Tom and Maria. Realizing I should have been paying closer attention to my stalker and everything else going on around me, I tell them I was concerned more about Jon dying and trying to figure out what to do next. Some of the things that happened seem to be bizarre at the time, but now that I think back on them . . . they were more than bizarre. They bordered on creepy and unsettling.

As a travel writer I have learned to pay close attention to everything around me. Somehow when Jon died, I forgot how to focus like that for a while. Now, my mind is more focused and I'm back to seeing everything clearly.

With that in mind, I tell Tom the morgue scene wasn't quite right. Even in my numbed state, things were off. I only saw Jon's face and only for a few moments. Not long. Plus, the policeman was . . . odd. Tom asks what I mean by odd. I tell him it was if he was an actor just playing a part. He didn't connect to me at all. And, I really don't think it was just me in shock. I don't know. I can't quite put my finger on it. He even overshadowed the doctor, now that I think back on it. But, strangely enough the doctor let him take that role.

While I'm talking, Tom is taking notes.

The funeral service was a blur. It all happened so quickly and I didn't even make any of the arrangements. At the time, I thought Mr. Jonse probably did . . . but I can't be sure about that. I was also in shock about the amount of money Jon left for me as well. That and the fact that I didn't know Jon had an attorney other than Mr. Fleetwood. I do remember calling Fleetwood's office shortly after Jon died and had a terrible conversation with his assistant. She was extremely rude, but that's about all I remember.

My travel purse, the one sitting here, is the one I always take on planes with me. It's always packed with my carry-on necessities and ready to go. I only need to add my passport, tickets, credit cards, and some money along with my travel journals, camera, tablet computer, cell phone, chargers, and batteries, and I'm ready.

Plus, it doesn't take me long to pack a suitcase with everything else I might need. I travel light and can be ready quickly. Jon was always amazed that I was packed before he was . . . and he was so much more organized than me. I smile, remembering our conversations about packing.

This was the bag I took to Mr. Jonse's office and to Barth's bank. I had just returned from Mexico and grabbed this one as it was larger than my small clutch bag. I wasn't sure what I would need to put in my purse from either Mr. Jonse's office or the safe deposit box, so the larger one made sense.

I tell Tom about the attempted break in while I was investigating Jon's hidden office in our home. The police came and looked around but found nothing unusual. I didn't think of it as odd at the time. It was just an attempted break in. Now, with everything else that's happened . . . it could have been related. It was right after I had the large envelope from Jon and was reading my way through it, starting with Jon's hidden office. I thought the envelope was part of the mail that came while I was in Mexico. Now that I think about it, I'm not positive it was mailed at all. It could have been hand delivered and my neighbor put it with my mail. I'm really not sure.

I've followed all of Jon's instruction to a 't' in those letters. Nothing else comes to mind, even when I try to think about every little detail. I do use my cell phone and keep it with me at all times.

I tell Tom that life has just been one strange issue after another since Jon died. Then it dawns on me. I don't think I ever mentioned the jewelry Jon left in the antique luggage piece from his office downtown.

75

As soon as I mention jewelry, I have Tom's attention. Once again, I head to my suite and retrieve the jewelry out of my safe. Maria tells me she noticed it the day I arrived and thought it was magnificent yet tasteful. I tell her I agree.

Tom looks at it carefully, turning it over and letting the light bounce off it. The more he looks, the more I'm seriously hoping it wasn't stolen. I would really hate to give it up. Yet, I don't want jewelry that doesn't belong to me.

It's so quiet I could hear the proverbial pin drop.

Finally, he looks at Maria, gives her my jewelry, and tells her to take a good look at the clasp.

Oh no . . .

When she's finished looking at it, they both look at me and Tom tells me he has another story for me. Am I ready for this?

Asking me if I remember the prince from Egypt with the gold bars, Tom continues. Well, the prince also had some gem stones stolen. Specifically, diamonds ranging from small to huge in size, with even larger emeralds. In fact, Jon recovered a small gray pouch along with the gold bars and didn't even look inside. When they returned the gold to the prince, they also handed him the pouch.

He opened it to reveal the largest stones either Tom or Jon had ever seen. Then he tried to give them some of the stones. Both flatly refused. The gold bars were more than enough. A few weeks later, Jon received a certified package from a well known jeweler with this necklace and ring. He contacted the prince and the prince told him to give it to his wife for a special occasion. Jon tried to say no, but the prince was adamant. Besides, he knows women love jewels. All of his women do . . .

When I ask Tom if I can legally keep them, he says they're mine. The gemstones in this necklace and ring were probably only one percent of the total stones in that pouch!

Wow . . .

Jon was apparently keeping the set to give to me on our anniversary. Shelly, his assistant, said he had the antique luggage case for a while. It would have been just like Jon to give me luggage . . . with jewelry inside. Now, these are even more special.

Tom asks me if there is anything else I may have forgotten.

When I tell him I really don't think so, he suggests we now head to Jon's other hidden room here at the villa. As we stand up, both he and Maria tell me that I must enter this room with an open mind. I must not jump to any conclusions when I see what is inside. There are reasons for everything. Some will be apparent and some I may never understand. Tom reminds me to bring my travel purse with me.

They're both scaring me with their intensity.

76

First of all, I have no idea where another room could possibly be located. I've been all over the villa exploring all the rooms, hallways, nooks, and crannies. Or so I thought. . . .

Exiting the den, we head toward the kitchen. This kitchen really is state of the art with every appliance any accomplished chef could ever want. From the six burner restaurant quality stove top to two oversized wall ovens, I could bake in here all day long. Both the refrigerator and freezer are filled with morsels I can't wait to sample. Cupboards hold tasteful, gorgeous Italian dinnerware and of course, an array of crystal wine glasses. These are in addition to crystal wine glasses and porcelain china I noticed in the wall cabinet in the dining room.

I love to cook and can't wait to try out some of the appliances I see here. I'm not a trained chef and I am not sure I want to cook for Jon's parents on their first night here, but then again . . . why not? Maria did say we would fix the meal together.

Along the back side are three walk-in pantries. Maria informs me one is completely stocked with food, one is for small appliances, and one contains larger pots and pans. Maria leads the way as we head for the pantry with the pots and pans. She turns and smiles at me. By now, I know for a fact she doesn't make wrong turns in this villa. She knows where every hidden spot is located. And, apparently every hidden room as well.

We all walk inside the pantry and Maria lifts a large stock pot off the shelf. If you weren't looking for it, you would never see the indentation in the shelf. It looks just like a rack the pot would sit on for storage. She removes a key from her pocket and inserts it into the rack. Immediately the pantry door we just entered closes and I hear a faint click. Tom explains that the door locked and now no one can enter this pantry from the kitchen.

Maria turns her key 45 degrees and the shelf swings open revealing a small hallway with a door. She steps aside and Tom enters a code into the panel on the wall. They both look at me and ask if I'm ready to see the rest of Jon's world.

Butterflies fill my stomach, my breathing becomes rapid, and I ask myself . . . what have I got to lose? Nodding nervously, I switch my travel purse from one shoulder to the other. Tom opens the door and leads the way into the room. I step through the doorway and immediately a loud, shrill siren goes off.

I think I scream.

77

Tom punches in a code on a second panel and the annoying siren stops. Silence. I'm not sure I can breathe. Maria takes my arm and guides me to a chair. Tom takes my travel purse from my shoulder and runs what appears to be similar to a TSA wand over it. It beeps like crazy. Maria and Tom look at each other.

Tom tells me he wants to look over my bag very carefully and I nod. Apparently I can now breathe . . . just not speak. He takes everything out and lays the contents on a glass table with a light under it. When he comes to the dark silver key ring with the small round gadget on it and lays it on the table, the light starts blinking rapidly. Looking at me, he asks where I got this key ring and I tell him the policeman at the morgue gave it to me and told me Jon had it in his pocket. I had actually forgotten it was in the bottom of my travel purse.

I told Tom, this wasn't one I recognized and I never did find the one I had given to Jon. But, since Jon had it in his pocket I figured it must have meant something to him. So, I didn't throw it away.

Tom wants me to confirm that I had never seen it before the policeman gave it to me.

I do.

Then, Tom lays it on the floor and smashes it with his foot. So much for keeping it. When he picks it up, he shows me what was inside. I shake my head and shrug my shoulders as I have no idea what he is showing me. He tells me it is a GPS tracking device.

What the hell? Who would want to track me?

Slowly I start putting pieces together.

Tom can see I am making sense of why things were happening around me. He says he assumes Barth had something to do with this, but he will have to check to see if anyone can confirm his suspicions.

Putting the broken pieces in his pocket, Tom tells me to stand up and look around the room. I had been so intent on the loud siren and then Tom finding the GPS that I didn't even look where we were or what was in Jon's room.

As my eyes sweep the room, I'm amazed, shocked, impressed, confused, and completely befuddled all at the same time. This looks like something out of a Star Trek adventure movie complete with a command post, big screens, blinking lights, maps, and wall monitors. With my mouth hanging open I turn to Maria and Tom. I don't get it.

Motioning for me to follow him, Tom tells me he will explain what each device is used for and what it does . . . for the most part. Then he tells me this special room was commissioned by a task force consisting of federal agencies from several different countries.

He had to get special clearance for me to even be in this room.

78

Tom begins . . . several years ago, he was part of a special task force that helped track some really bad people. He can't tell me specifics but he can tell me a few of things they were doing. Apparently, these people buy airplanes and then don't pay for them. These are expensive planes, upwards of several million dollars each. Some of these people use those planes for illegal acts. These range from smuggling both people and goods to kidnapping and murder.

I nod my head in astonishment and listen.

Continuing . . . Tom says one particular group of people from Russia were promising young girls modeling careers. They would pay them an advance, take their photos, and fly them to a nice hotel in London. Then they would promise them a trip before their modeling careers took off. At this point, the girls had no choice but to go with these men. These trips took the girls to unsavory places where they were then turned into sex slaves. Or worse yet, some were sold for very sick escapades.

Now my skin is beginning to crawl.

Tom tells me there were all sorts of criminals being sought by every federal agency in the world. He asks me if I remember him talking about Fortini.

Right. The man who originally put Tom and Jon in touch with recovering stolen art.

Well . . . Tom pauses and I know I'm about to learn something more.

Fortini's uncle, the one who owned this villa, along with a couple of other uncles and Fortini's father were part of the Italian Mafia at one time. As my eyes get larger, Tom assures me I have nothing to worry about. Yeah, right . . .

This room has always been here; it was built into the original plans for this villa. Its purpose was then the same as what it is being used for today. Surveillance. Only, back then, the surveillance was more like a group of guys sitting around a table with wine and cigars telling each other who was going to take care of whom and how.

Now, it gets used by different agencies when they want a secure place for communications. Most of the time, no one actually comes to this room; it's used to monitor activities. But, if Tom or Jon needed to contact someone in a totally secure manner . . . this is where they would do the contacting. And, if they need hi-tech communication tools . . . this is where they would come.

Questioningly, I look at Maria. She tells me she has used this room to monitor activities when she was involved in recovery projects or to handle correspondence that she didn't want anyone to know about.

Still not sure what she's talking about, I nod. Then I ask them both if I will ever need to access this room. Probably not, they tell me.

Right now, Tom is more concerned about the GPS from my bag. A few minutes ago he put in a call when he walked to one of the machines. As it now beeps, Tom goes to one of the monitors and picks up a headset device. As he talks to someone, Maria tells me that Tom is good at his job. Probably as good as anybody in this business. I ask if Tom is a spy.

Not really . . . she tells me.

79

Tom comes back to us and says he has positive confirmation that the GPS device was indeed one of Barth's.

When I ask how he can tell, he just says to trust him. And, I do.

Apparently, we can now conclude that Barth was tracking me. When I ask if this had to do with the jewelry his sister stole from the hotel safe in Paris years ago, Tom believes it does. They have also learned the concierge at that hotel was related to Barth and his sister. This concierge was also instrumental in arranging other hotel robberies for Barth. No one connected him as he changed his name and appearance every time he applied to work in a new hotel.

Barth must have figured Jon shared everything with me and that I knew where the necklace was hidden. Tom goes on to say that the policemen who found Jon were legitimate policemen. But, the policeman at the hospital morgue was not. He was probably another one of Barth's hired men. However, the doctor was legitimate and probably just being polite to the pushy policeman.

That was the policeman who gave me the plastic bag with the things from Jon's pockets. He was probably hoping I would keep it in my purse or at least close to me.

The man Tom was just talking to about the GPS, told Tom the so called policeman was found floating in the Pacific Ocean by Bodega Bay a few weeks ago. An abandoned sailboat was found nearby, so it was originally assumed he had a sailing accident. After more investigation, authorities discovered he was shot at close range. No one has claimed the body, but a search on some federal database found that he used to work for Barth as a guard at his bank.

It's all beginning to add up, Tom tells me. Barth wanted the jewelry, he wanted to hurt Jon, and apparently he wanted revenge for something that was only in his mind. He truly was crazy.

We exit the tech room the same way we entered. With a sigh of relief that another chapter is complete, I feel like things will get back to somewhat normal for me.

Tom and Maria ask if I'm okay.

When I tell them I'm still trying to absorb how Jon could have been mixed up in all this and that I never had a clue, Tom looks at me and says he knows why.

Why?

Jon was good . . . no, he was excellent at what he did. So, I ask Tom . . . was Jon a spy?

Not really. . . .

80

Peter and Diane will be here tomorrow and Maria and I need to start preparing for the meals. But, right now I want to sit in the garden and think about everything I've learned. Telling Maria I will help her in a little while, she shoos me out of the kitchen and tells me to enjoy the late afternoon sunlight. Dinner is ready to go into the oven, so she is going to check on her pets and possibly take a nap.

Tom has disappeared.

As I sit and listen to the gently bubbling fountain and let the late sun warm my face, I'm back to thinking about my life with Jon. The wonderful life Jon and I had together wasn't an act . . . was it? We really did enjoy traveling together, each other's company, and discovering new things . . . didn't we? I know I was happy. I think Jon was, too. I loved our trips exploring all parts of the world. I'm pretty sure Jon enjoyed those as well.

In the back of my mind, I always wondered about Jon's childhood. But, it was obvious he didn't want to talk about it so I didn't pressure him. The only thing I knew about his parents was that they gave us money to buy our house in San Francisco. For all I knew, they could have died years ago. Guess I was way off base on that. Now that I know they are well-known artists and lead very private lives, I understand why Jon was as private about them as he was. I do wonder if they can fill me in on any details about Jon's childhood. Did he always want to be an engineer? Did he always love puzzles and turn everything he did into one?

Smiling, I remember many discussions where I would have a problem with a travel article or a photo. Jon would look at what I was doing and tell me to look at it a different way. To him, it was so simple. It was just another puzzle to be solved.

No wonder he was so good at this spy stuff. Even if he wasn't really a spy . . .

I should get out my journals and start taking some more notes. I do believe most of my questions have been answered, though. Nothing seems to be missing as Tom and Maria helped put all the pieces in order for me. Now, I just need to decide what I'm going to do next and where I'm going to spend the rest of my life. I need to contact the magazine and make arrangements with them. I know I would never have to work again, but I don't really think of myself as the retired type. But, I'm not the jetsetter type, either.

Plus, I really need to do something that holds my interest. That would be traveling and writing. Hmm, I think to myself . . . maybe I should start my own magazine or travel company.

I remember when my parents retired and moved to Lake Tahoe, they wondered if they would like spending all their time there. They thought about being retired and what that meant to them.

Hmm . . . I hadn't thought about them in a long time. With all the things that have happened I really wonder if they were involved in an accident or whether Barth could have had something to do with their deaths as well. I guess at this point it doesn't really matter. Barth is dead and I can honestly say I'm glad of that.

The sun has set, the lights have come on in the gardens, and it's time to get ready for dinner. Tomorrow I meet Jon's parents.

81

Our dinner conversation covered a wide variety of topics, starting once again with Jon's death. I ask Tom and Maria if Jon's parents know how he was killed and if they know all the events surrounding me since then.

Tom has told them Jon was killed so they know he did not have a heart attack. They know about recovering the paintings Barth stole but that's about it. They didn't ask many questions of Tom and he didn't alarm them with any more of the details of the ugliness in the past few months.

Peter still paints but not nearly as much as he used to and Diane doesn't sculpt much anymore either. They prefer to manage the galleries while they encourage new artists. Both of them conduct workshops several times a year, mostly in London and Florence. They still reside in Austria and they continue to keep that private from the workshops. They have started foundations for beginning artists and they like their lives as they are. Tom thinks I will really enjoy them and Maria agrees. Once again, it's too bad it's under these circumstances that I finally get to meet my in-laws.

Then I ask Tom why they had never wanted to meet me before. I think it's strange, considering Jon was their only child.

He tells me there is a little more to that story. Remember the attempt on Jon's nanny's life, he asks me? When I tell him yes, he says that there were several other threats on their lives as well. They became paranoid enough that they didn't leave their home for quite some time. Then, Jon started in this business with Tom. That allowed him to go to their home to see them. He always had photos of me with him, Tom tells me. They saw me, but I never saw them.

Tom pauses, as if to add more . . . but doesn't.

Growing up the way Jon did still seems strange to me, but I guess that's the way it had to be.

Our conversation moves on to Barth and everything he touched. We all believe he really was crazy and probably clinically psychotic. His obsession with Jon is something we will never really understand. He had never been married and had no kids, thank goodness. It seems all of his hired thugs are either behind bars or dead.

When I ask Tom what will happen to his bank, Tom tells me it has already been handed over to the appropriate authorities and customers are being informed.

And, the private room in the basement?

The paintings I saw, or thought I saw, were real. They were stolen from Peter's gallery in London. They are in the process of being returned to the London gallery. Wow. He really did have an obsession with Jon.

Remember those guards at the bank? They were with Barth on his fishing boat in Baja and were killed as well. Speculation has it that it was a murder, suicide . . . just not sure who shot who first. It seems the weapon was recovered on the boat.

Tom's just not sure this scenario plays out in his mind. It's much too clean and staged for his liking. But, on the other hand . . . they are dead and can't hurt anyone anymore.

Mr. Jonse has been in the loop with Jon and Tom throughout the entire recovery business.

Shortly, our conversation turns back to me. What am I going to do? Telling both of them I was just having that same conversation with myself in the garden, I am starting to work on some plans. I am not ready to retire. I will continue to travel and write, but I've thought about starting my own travel magazine or even a travel company.

Maria thinks both are great ideas and she would be willing to help me in any way she can. She has a friend who works for a fashion magazine and is ready to get out of that particular industry. Maybe she would be a good resource if I start the travel magazine. Then, she asks me why I wouldn't combine them into one company.

Hmm . . . great idea.

About midnight we all decide it's time to get some sleep. It's been another eventful day. Asking Tom what is going to happen to the special room here, he tells me it will remain functional in case he needs to use it. He is retiring from the stolen art recovery business but will continue to act as a consultant for various agencies if they need him. It's time for him to settle down in one place.

When I ask if he was ever married, he looks at Maria and then tells me it's not something he usually talks about.

Pausing, Tom tells me he was engaged about a year and a half ago but his finance was killed in a strange accident.

What? How many of these strange accidents have I heard about in the last six months?

He continues . . . she was skiing with friends in the Alps and an avalanche overtook them. They were all killed. The snow was so deep, they never recovered their bodies. He was supposed to be with them, but at the last minute ended up working on an art heist. He's often thought about Barth and wondered if he had anything to do with her death.

Then he looks at me and says there's more . . .

She was Jon's sister.

82

What?

Okay . . . who can sleep now? Asking for another glass of wine, I tell him I need to know more. This is just too bizarre. Jon had a sister?

Tom settles himself in the chair and begins to tell me this part of Jon's story.

Remember the attempt on Jon's nanny's life? Again, I say yes. I've heard this part before. Not really, says Tom. Not only was the nanny taking care of six year old Jon but also of his newborn baby sister, Heidi.

When the attempt happened, Jon went off to boarding school the following year and Heidi was cared for by Diane's mother in Paris until she was old enough to attend boarding school, too. No one knew Diane's mother so the arrangement worked out perfectly. Periodically, both Jon and Heidi would come to visit Austria by way of some other country. Peter and Diane were very careful.

And it worked. No other attempts were made and things seemed to be some sort of normal for them.

Ahh . . . I'm beginning to see how Jon and Heidi grew up.

I tell Tom I wish I could have met her. He tells me she was at our wedding but Peter and Diane did not want her to announce who she was.

Seriously? At our wedding and I didn't know it?

She was one of the photographers, Tom tells me. She was just starting out in the photography world, and weddings weren't really her forte. She was into nature photography. My goodness.

Our photos were excellent and Jon wanted to hire the photographers, which was okay with me.

Tom tells me she inherited her eye for art, light, and image from both parents. She studied for years in many mediums and was becoming a well-known nature photographer shortly before she was killed by the avalanche.

Can I really digest all of this? Jon's parents have endured so much. I really can't wait to meet them tomorrow. It's like I know all about them but yet know nothing at all.

83

Surprisingly, I had a great night's sleep. I would have thought my brain wouldn't have slowed down long enough to let me sleep at all. Well rested, shower finished, and ready for a new day, I head to the kitchen to grab some delicious Italian coffee and help Maria with dinner preparations for tonight.

She tells me Jon's parents will be here mid-afternoon. She has already prepared an antipasto plate for our afternoon snack and has also chosen the wine. Directing me to set out the appropriate dishes and wine glasses, I do as I'm told. We both are looking forward to their arrival.

Tom lets us know the authorities are here to remove some of the stolen pieces from the special storage room; the room I saw when I first arrived. Everything has been documented and the owners are awaiting the return of their art. Then he hands me a check.

What the hell! It's for $100,000. Staring at Tom with my mouth hanging open, I shake my head in bewilderment.

He informs me it is the reward for just one of the paintings. The Picasso is worth many, many times more than that. I tell him I didn't do anything to earn this and he says, 'Jon did'. When I suggest the three of us split it, he and Maria let me know they have earned other checks just as large in the last couple of weeks. That same heist had more than just one expensive piece of art. This check is entirely mine.

Whoa. It almost looks like play money, but Tom assures me the cashier's check is very real.

Since Tom is going into town to deposit his checks, he offers to deposit this one for me. I didn't know I had a bank account in town. He explains it is connected to my bank in the United States. Mr. Jonse has everything set up so Jon or I could deposit and withdraw anywhere in the world.

Nice . . . I think.

Tom leaves and we continue preparing dinner. Maria asks if I've given any more thought to developing a travel magazine or travel business.

Actually, I tell her, I started forming a business plan in my head but that was about as far as I got with it. She suggests that we brainstorm and work on it after Jon's parents leave.

Which reminds me to ask her . . . how long are they staying?

She thinks they plan on staying only two or three days. They need to be in Florence for a workshop Diane is conducting a week from today. She knows they like to arrive early for those to make sure everything is set up the way they want it.

They notified her earlier their driver would not be staying here with them. He has other plans and will come back to pick them up when they are ready to leave. She tells me the guest suites are ready in case they each want their own suite. Which brings up another question . . . do we have a cleaning lady? Do I need to help clean? I certainly don't mind.

Maria tells me there is a young girl that comes every morning while we are eating breakfast to pick up, clean up, and take care of anything she sees that needs attention. She must be good. I've never seen or heard her. And, now that I think about it, I've wondered why everything is so clean in my suite. I'm neat . . . but things are spotless when I return to it during the day. I knew it wasn't magic.

Maria and I continue to work while we chat. Tom returns and we all sit down for lunch. Afterwards, we all go our separate ways, anticipating the arrival of Peter and Diane.

After freshening up in my suite, I take a journal with me to one of the back gardens. Maria's pets entertain me while I start to work on my business plan. Chew is rolling in the grass while inspecting butterflies, bouncing as he walks. Mo stalks a bird for a while then, deciding that's too much work, stretches out in the sun for a cat nap.

Around the edge of the patio, Maria comes running toward me, waving her arms, and looking like she's seen a ghost. I've never seen her so frazzled. She can hardly speak. Breathlessly she tells me to take a deep breath and follow her. I need to come quickly.

Peter and Diane are here and there's a problem.

84

Slightly alarmed, I follow Maria, trying to catch up with her. She moves fast when she wants.

Rounding the corner, I see the front of the villa where an awesome Mercedes is parked. A uniformed driver is helping a woman out of the back seat. I know I'm several feet away but as she stands up and turns my way, I think to myself she certainly appears too young to be Jon's mother. Then I see Maria hugging another older woman and man; first one, then the other. They are all gesturing and smiling. Maria still looks flustered.

As I get closer, Maria rushes over to me. Goodness, she's like a little hummingbird. I have not seen this side of her. Telling me Peter and Diane have news, she takes my hand and introduces me to Jon's parents.

I'm amazed at how much Jon looked and acted like Peter. His build, the shape of his forehead, the way he shook my hand . . . everything. But, Jon definitely inherited his mother's smile. She greeted me warmly, smiling the whole time. There is so much I want to ask and so much I want to tell them. Later . . .

Maria turns as the younger woman approaches. She is just as striking as Diane, but tall like Peter. She also has Diane's dazzling smile. Maria gestures to Peter and he introduces her as their daughter, Heidi.

I think I need to sit down. Where is Tom?

85

Once I am able to find my words, I welcome them to my villa. At least I think I closed my mouth.

Maria has recovered by now and invites everyone in, directing their driver where to put their luggage. I just follow along, still not believing what I'm seeing. Peter recognizes that I'm still in shock and puts his arm around my shoulders. He informs me he has many things to tell us but he wants Tom in the room as well.

I'm certainly glad we decided to have wine with our afternoon antipasto platter. Hopefully, we have several bottles.

Diane says she would like to freshen up before we sit down to chat and Heidi agrees. They follow the driver upstairs to their suites, telling us they will both be back in a few minutes. Maria goes to find Tom and Peter stays with me as we head to the terrace off the dining room.

I'm amazed I can even walk. Recently finding out that Jon had a sister is one thing. But, seeing Heidi, after Tom told us she died a year and a half ago, is quite another shock.

I pick up a bottle of wine from the chiller and the glasses I put out earlier today. Was that really only this morning? Peter opens the wine and tells me he feels like he knows me, as he offers a toast.

He tells me Jon kept him informed about our lives and they very much wanted to meet with us so many times. He just couldn't be sure that everyone would be safe. He'll fill me in a little more on some recent events when everyone else is here.

For now, he wants to know if I'm okay. Then he asks me what my plans are for the future. He is so comfortable to talk to and I find myself telling him about my travel magazine or possibly a travel business. I have so many ideas that I started a journal to help me decide. He tells me he has a person that could help me with my plans and he'll introduce us later.

Thanking him, I tell him he reminds me so much of Jon. When he chuckles and shrugs his shoulders, I tell him that's exactly what Jon would have done. We chat a little more as Maria and Tom make their way to the terrace. Tom had been finalizing the return of the Picasso and filing all the necessary paperwork. He still has no idea about Heidi being alive and being here.

Maria pours some wine and gets out the food. Tom and Peter greet each other, Tom asks about their trip, and then Tom asks about Diane. As if on cue, Diane returns from her suite and opens the door to the terrace. Tom turns to greet Diane with a kiss on both cheeks. Heidi steps around Diane and Tom turns white.

86

From ashen to red in less than a blink of the eye, Tom looks at Peter, then back to Heidi in disbelief. I can't tell if he's in shock, slightly miffed, or really, really angry. Peter takes his arm and hands him a glass of wine. He asks Tom to hear him out before he reacts. Tom can ask questions when he's finished. Then Peter asks Heidi and Diane to have a seat.

Tom starts to protest and Peter quietly asks him to listen. We all sit and stare at Peter. Diane has a forced smile on her face and Heidi looks alternately at Peter and at her lap glancing once in a while over at Tom. Peter starts by telling Tom he has every right to hate them all. No kidding, I think to myself.

When Heidi was caught in the avalanche, the rescue squad found her and one other person alive but both critically injured. The doctors weren't sure either one of them was going to make it to the hospital or survive the multiple surgeries once they arrived. They tried to alert Tom but he was undercover and unavailable. Tom nods as if remembering that.

Heidi came through all of the major rounds of surgeries but had to be placed in a drug induced coma. The doctors said it was the best way for her to recover from her internal injuries and planned to wake her up gradually over the next few days. This is where it gets scary, Peter tells us.

Heidi looks at Tom who looks as if he's ready to kill a bear . . . with his bare hands.

The other person found alive, a boyfriend of one of Heidi's friends, woke up from surgery the following day and told the doctors he was sorry. He told them he didn't know anyone would die. He really didn't want to hurt Heidi but there was no other way. Figuring he was still reacting to the medication, they told him they understood and asked him to relax.

He became agitated and asked who survived the avalanche. When they told him just he and Heidi survived, he broke down sobbing and babbling. A nurse was just about to give him an injection to knock him out when he started speaking more clearly. What he said caused the doctors to contact the authorities.

By now, he was coherent and had quite the story to tell. He told them the avalanche was rigged and it was supposed to only kill Heidi. He didn't want it that way. But, 'they' assured him his girlfriend would be okay and they would wire the money to him once he cleared the avalanche. He figured he could save Heidi, he figured his girlfriend and he could make it look like Heidi was killed, and he figured they could get Heidi to safety. Never once did he think anyone would actually get killed. He can't believe his girlfriend didn't survive and tells the police he feels responsible.

The police talked with him at length, making note of all his details surrounding the men who contacted him and who gave him the money. They assured him he didn't kill his girlfriend. He didn't believe them.

A week later he killed himself. Heidi recovered enough to go to the villa in Austria for extensive rehabilitation.

87

When Tom starts to ask a question, Peter tells him he wants to finish the story. He informs him that Tom can then do whatever he wants to him.

Heidi continued to get physically stronger over the last year. She now walks without a cane, most of her scars have healed nicely, she has a clean bill of health from all of her physicians and her therapists, and only about a month ago did she start taking photos again.

There was a problem, however.

Not uncommon in major accidents, Heidi suffers from a severe form of amnesia. Throughout the past few months her memory has begun to return and she now can remember most of her life before the accident. However, she has no memory of the accident or the avalanche. She probably never will. The last thing she remembers is at the top of the ski slope, when they all talked about who was cooking dinner once they made it back to their lodge.

She still becomes sad when she thinks about no one else surviving. And, she's sad that her friend's boyfriend felt he had to take his own life after surviving the avalanche.

At Heidi's last appointment, she finally asked about Tom. The doctors wanted her to remember him on her own and didn't want to send her back into shock if he just showed up to see her. When she finally did ask about him, Peter and Diane decided it was time to notify Tom. Then, all this business with Jon happened and they decided to wait. They weren't sure if Heidi would be safe or if there were going to be more attempts on her life. Was the madness starting all over again?

The goal was to bring Tom to Austria. But, that plan was put on hold.

Then, once they were notified who was behind the avalanche, all the attempts on their lives, and everything surrounding it, they could finally relax. Joseph Barth, III and his thugs were now out of the picture. For good.

When I watched Tom during Peter's story, his facial muscles relaxed and he appeared less angry looking. Now, he was looking directly at Heidi and she back at him. It certainly appears they will be okay and may be able to start over.

Tom asks Heidi a few questions as we all move to the dining room. Maria and I head to the kitchen to bring the next course. Peter joins us and opens another bottle of wine.

Back in the dining room, Tom and Heidi are engrossed in catching up on each other. Tom, of course, wants specifics. Heidi is just glad to be alive and back in one piece.

She asks if he wants to see her scars and Peter groans.

88

orning came quickly. We all must have stayed up half the night talking and putting all the pieces together for everyone. It seems all of us knew most of the story but the only one who knew it all was Peter. He filled us in on the beginning with Barth. That's the part that the rest of us just didn't know about.

It happened a long time ago, starts Peter. There was Joseph Barth, Joseph Barth, Jr., and Joseph Barth, III . . . Peter explains.

Talk about confusing . . . Now I know that Joseph Barth, III is the one I had contact with at the bank.

Peter's father and Joseph Barth, Jr. knew each other, in a strange way. Mr. Jonse had told me about Barth, Jr. and that he wasn't a model citizen. Peter confirmed that and more by telling us that when Barth, Jr. inherited the money from his father, he used it just as poorly as his own father had. Apparently, it was quite a large sum of money plus the bank.

Barth, Jr. had some friends that were legitimate art collectors. He tried several times to bid on some art at auctions, but was always outbid. That didn't set well with him so he resorted to what he thought was the next best way to obtain the art. He arranged for it to be stolen. Only, he didn't really know anything about art. He just knew he wanted famous paintings. The next display and auction was to be held in Switzerland. Barth, Jr. was going to have some art, one way or another.

Peter's father was young and just starting out as president of a major bank in Geneva. Joseph Barth, Jr. was older and upset he didn't have the art collection to match his much younger friends.

One evening right before the auction, Peter's father and mother were at a gala celebrating the auction. This auction was to be the event of the year. Countless galas, dinners, and pre-auction events were being held. Peter's father started talking to a man who introduced himself as new to the art collecting world. He asked many interesting questions at first. When the questions became more about security surrounding the art and if he knew how well it was guarded, Peter's father tried to change the subject. That didn't work for long and the questions came back to security, guards, and when the art was going to be ready for viewing. With his radar in full gear, he sidestepped most questions, giving answers that weren't quite true.

Peter's father excused himself and contacted the head of security. Since much of the art was being stored in a huge vault in the bank where Peter's father was president, he knew much more than he told Barth, Jr.

You can probably guess what happened that night. Barth, Jr. and two hired thieves tried to enter the bank through an elaborate labyrinth of tunnels. Security was purposely turned off in order to catch them in the act. It worked and all three were apprehended.

Somehow Barth, Jr. discovered who he had been talking to that night. Or, possibly he knew it all along. It's hard to tell. When the thieves were being transported to a prison in Switzerland awaiting extradition to the United States, all three were found hanged in their cells. Barth, Jr's son, Joseph Barth, III, grew up knowing this story. He wanted revenge on everyone connected to his father's death.

The more revenge he wanted, the more psychotic he became.

As Peter was telling this story, I thought back to my brief encounter with Joseph Barth, III at his bank in San Francisco. He was as crazy as his father. I shuddered at what could have happened. No wonder I had a gut feeling about him.

Now, as we all sat enjoying our coffee on the terrace, Peter looks directly at me. Asking me if I can handle all this . . . the history, Jon, this villa, the drama, and life from now on . . . I tell him I can finally deal with everything that has happened in the last few months.

I tell him it seems like a lifetime ago that Jon and I were planning our anniversary trip. Yet, it seems like only yesterday. I guess that's the way it is. I will move on with my life without Jon.

I tell him I don't think anything else will ever shock me the way these past few months have. And, I'm so glad I finally met him and Diane.

Peter takes my hands, looks even more intently at me, and tells me, "Wait here."

Epilogue

Overlooking the Grand Canal in Venice, I sit on the balcony sipping Venetian Spritz and watching all the activity. I can't believe any of it. I can't believe it's only been a week since Peter looked at me on the terrace at the villa and told me, "Wait here."

I can't believe the events from then on. I just can't believe it.

To fill you in . . . Jon was indeed shot. He was shot either by Joseph Barth, III or by one of his thugs. The so called policeman at the morgue was indeed on Barth's payroll and not a real policeman. However, the doctor in the morgue was a real doctor who had some suspicions about the policeman and the way he was acting toward me. He convinced the policeman Jon was dead and that he, the doctor, needed to contact the funeral home. Apparently that was good enough for the policeman, who left Jon's body at the hospital.

But, Jon was not dead. He and Tom had been tipped off about several events and had started wearing protective gear . . . Kevlar type vests. So, he wasn't even seriously wounded. But, the policeman didn't know that.

Once Jon was awake, he contacted the FBI. Since everyone, from the FBI to Interpol, was looking for a way to pin several murders and major thefts on Joseph Barth, III, they convinced Jon to let everyone believe he was dead . . . including me.

When Peter told me on the terrace to "Wait here," he then said he had a surprise for me. Asking me if I could handle a major shock, I seriously had no idea what could even bring this level of seriousness to his face. I was curious and a little apprehensive all at the same time.

Peter then asked me to stay sitting and that he would be right back.

When he entered the terrace this time, he had his arm around Jon. Someone screamed . . . I'm sure it was me. To my credit I didn't faint but I couldn't stand up on my own either. Jon grabbed me and just held on. I have no idea how long we stood like that.

When we finally sat down, everyone else had gone inside. I just stared at Jon, mouth hanging open, tears of joy running down my cheeks.

Jon explained what he had been doing since then, working undercover with many different law enforcement agencies, using many different aliases. Everything has finally been all wrapped up. Everyone that was involved in Barth's elaborate theft ring has been caught or is dead. Barth's bank has been completely divested, with all the legitimate customers receiving their monies. Jon has officially retired from the art and jewelry recovery business.

One more thing he says he needs for me to know . . .

Can I handle knowing something about my husband that might bother me? Not sure what he could possibly tell me that would surprise me more than anything in the last six months . . . I say sure.

Why not?

Jon tells me he was the one who killed Joseph Barth, III and the two thugs on the yacht just off Baja.

About the Author

WENDY VANHATTEN, owner of VanHatten Writing Services, is a published author, the editor of Prime Time Living Magazine, and a contributing author for several magazines. She has taught writing at the college level and travel writing workshops. Her children's books, the Max and Myron series, teach children to read while developing good character traits. Currently, she documents travel advice and photos in her blog at www.travelsandescapes.blogspot.com. Other ventures include her Writing Concierge Service for authors and her Crazy Girls Cookies, the fun piece of her work (www.crazygirlscookies.com) where she interacts with bakeries and people from all over the world. Her books may be found on Amazon or from her website, www.wendyvanhatten.com

ADDITIONAL TITLES BY
WENDY VANHATTEN

My Life: The Sequel: A Girlfriend's Guide to Personal Success
When the Cat Speaks...Listen A purr...fectly good way to enjoy life
Dad's Hidden Box

MAX & MYRON SERIES
by Wendy VanHatten and R David Kryder with illustrations by Corie Barloggi

Max and Myron Learn Please and Thank You
Max and Myron, My First Day of School
Max and Myron I'm Sorry, Please Forgive Me
Max & Myron Learn Please Don't Tease
Max & Myron Learn Big and Small, Short and Tall

The Authorship Journey: A profitable adventure? by Wendy Vanhatten, Ginger Marks, Misty Taggart, and Tracee Gleichner

Available on Amazon.com and fine bookstores everywhere.

www.ingramcontent.com/pod-product-compliance
Lightning Source LLC
Chambersburg PA
CBHW050417260626
47156CB00003B/1051